THE LAW BEHIND THE GUN

From Nebraska to Nevada was a twenty-seven-day ride for a man on the trail of his brother's killer. But arrival in Nevada was not the end of the trail. First, before a slain boy could be avenged, there were the men and methods of Nevada's powerful Keystone cow-outfit to be overcome; there was a gutted town to be paid for; and the trail of fleeing kill___ __ __ _____ _ ___ ____ and scarl___

This _____ attle agai___ __ ____ _un actio___ ___ __un-man___

THE LAW BEHIND
THE GUN

THE LAW BEHIND THE GUN

by
James Glenn

MAGNA PRINT BOOKS
Long Preston, North Yorkshire,
England.

British Library Cataloguing in Publication Data.

Glenn, James, *1916—*
   The law behind the gun.

   ISBN 1-85057-699-8 pbk

First Published in Great Britain by Robert Hale Ltd. 1962.

Copyright © 1962 by James Glenn

Published in Large Print 1989 by arrangement with Robert Hale Ltd., London

Printed and bound in Great Britain by
Redwood Burn Limited, Trowbridge, Wiltshire.

60556

CHAPTER ONE

There was a pleasant liveliness to the scent which passed into the room from an open window. The fragrance of rain before any rain fell.

Beyond the window Kearney lay in its depthless mantle of light, moon-shadowed and silhouetted, with the black-cut of the Wasatch Range looming even darker off to the north.

Nevada in the springtime, thought the man standing in that darkened room looking out, was a little like a woman. All the hardness, the cruelty and deceit, were for a time softened, rounded, made warmly inviting. But only for a time. Nevada was a desert, and if it had any genuine softness or roundness he had not found it.

He shifted position, moved a little closer to the window but not too close because he wished to see but he did not wish to be seen.

Nevada was a thousand miles of nothing. Some of it was tilted on edge, some of it was as flat as that grave he had visited in wintery Nebraska, and all of it was wasteland; waterless, sterile, and covered with an alkaline, powder-fine dust that rose up to itch a man's hide and burn his eyes.

He made a cigarette and stuck it, unlit, between his lips. The towns of Nevada were ugly too, he thought; they were square and unpainted and strictly functional. Take Kearney for example: There was one roadway, maybe a hundred feet wide. It was a regular quagmire when it rained and for the ten months of the year when there was no rain it was ankle-thick in dust. And the buildings, they were all alike, square, weathered, warped, unpainted. Even with springtime's sparkling days and beautiful nights the buildings still looked grim, inhospitable and ugly.

Nevada might be, as he had been told, good cow country, but so far he had seen nothing to tempt him, even now; even in the springtime when new life was coming out of the ground, and the good sap was running strong again, Nevada couldn't begin to compare with Nebraska.

He shielded his face and lit the cigarette, sucked back a lungful of smoke and let it out slowly. Twenty-seven days on the trail wearied a man to the marrow. Maybe that was why he couldn't see anything good about Nevada.

A fork-tongued flash of far-off lightning crackled across the heavens, and in that steel-grey second he saw the horseman across the road turn, run a long gaze up the roadway and turn away again facing the saloon. It was all the time he needed to recognise that face.

It was more gaunt than he remembered it, and the dark clothing was dusty from travel. He smiled without mirth; the man across the road had been even longer on the trail. When a man is running he loses a little weight and he gets a little tarnished-looking; haunted-looking, the stranger to Kearney thought from his position in the darkened hotel room. It was the price a man paid for living as that man lived.

He put out the cigarette, took up his hat and moved through the darkness to the door. Beyond, in the ghostly corridor, he slow-paced his way to the lobby, across it and emerged upon the plankwalk with all the sights and sounds of Kearney around him.

Across the roadway orange lamplight struck downward into the dust and lay there in a warm square. Dark-squared silhouettes of moving men glided through the night upon that far plankwalk. Invariably they turned in at the saloon.

The stranger shifted his cartridge belt unconsciously and squinted ahead where a black-white sign shone dimly. 'Kearney's Palace of

Pleasure' the sign said. He smiled, stepped down into the dust and cut across to the far walkway. There, he hesitated a moment to throw a calculating glance both ways before pushing on into the saloon.

Somewhere from beyond the press of shifting bodies a woman's voice came to him low and hard. It stayed with him like a fragment of music; inviting, pleasant, promising.

He leaned upon the wall near the door to make another cigarette. He had no urge to smoke but a cigarette could be utilised for other things too. He studied the room.

There were perhaps thirty men between the bar and card tables. They seemed to be fully at ease. He thought, in a place like Kearney, Nevada, everyone knew everyone else. There was the laughter, the cat-calls, the banter one heard in almost every cowtown saloon he'd ever been in, where the riders all knew one another.

He lit the cigarette and dropped his match. The man he wanted was standing at the bar talking to a brace of cowmen. In this better light his face seemed even more gaunt-looking than it had outside in the roadway. A third cowman came up and joined the conversation. He slapped the gaunt man on the shoulder and dust flew. In a hearty voice he boomed: 'By golly, Mike, it's been quite a spell. Where you been anyway?'

The gaunt man made some kind of reply but it was indistinguishable. He did not see the stranger watching him, but it wouldn't have mattered if he had because he did not know him by sight. By reputation maybe, but not by sight.

The stranger smoked a while longer, then turned silently and passed back out into the night. He knew something now which made it necessary to change his plans. He had intended to walk in, call the gaunt man out and shoot him. He had been on the trail twenty-seven days with that one thought uppermost in his mind. Now though, it would have to be done in a different way because obviously the gaunt man was home. He evidently had either lived in Kearney before going down to the Nebraska plains, or perhaps had originally come from Kearney. In either case if a stranger rode in one day, killed the gaunt man the next day, his chances of riding out the third day would be pretty slim. People had a way of being antagonistic about strangers killing their friends.

Well, he told himself, a bath, a big feed at the café down the road a piece from the hotel, maybe a drink or two afterwards then a good night's sleep were what he needed more than

11

anything else anyway. Mike could wait. Mike Barlow, the killer of an eighteen-year-old kid named Bucky Wheeler could wait another few days. He was twenty-seven bitter days from Blockton, Nebraska, too, and he also needed a little rest. This brought another little smile to the stranger's lips. Maybe Mike thought he was safe now. Maybe because he was back among friends he didn't think Bucky Wheeler's notorious gun-fighting brother Bob Wheeler would find him, or if he did find him, would risk calling him out in his own town.

He was still smiling when the hotel clerk saw him coming and smiled too. 'What can I do for you, Mr Smith?'

'I want a bath.'

'Sure, Mr Smith. I'll have the swamper haul the water. That'll be two bits extra.'

"Mr Smith" put a coin upon the counter. 'Call me when the bath's ready,' he said, and crossed to a chair, dropped heavily down and half-closed his eyes. It was good to be at the end of the trail; it was also good to sit relaxed in a chair after so long a time in the saddle. He let his lids fully down, and after what seemed no more than a moment but which was actually half an hour he opened them again, jarred into full wakefulness by a man's voice. It was not the clerk either; it was a large man with sharp

12

blue eyes, a high-bridged nose and a long, thin mouth. A cowman, Wheeler thought, sizing him up, and a successful one too, if clothing meant anything.

'You must be doggoned tired,' the big man said, holding his cool, appraising gaze fully on the younger man's face.

'I am,' the gunfighter replied evenly, until then unaware of a second man, not so tall and quite a few years younger, standing diffidently behind the cowman. 'And you must be pretty hard up for someone to talk—to wake people up you don't know, mister.'

The cowman's still gaze hardened. 'My name is Cullen,' he said. 'Does that mean anything to you?'

'Not a thing, Mr Cullen.'

'I own the Keystone.'

Wheeler yawned, flicked the second man a short look, then stood up. 'Good for you,' he drawled. 'Now tell me something, Mr Cullen—just what in hell is the Keystone?'

The second man stirred. His voice, when he spoke, sounded boyish. 'Keystone is the biggest cow outfit in Nevada, stranger, and Mr Cullen is one of the richest men between here and the Missouri River.'

Bob Wheeler studied Cullen over a moment of silence then nodded in acknowledgment of this oblique introduction. 'All right,' he said. 'Now tell me why you woke me up.'

'The clerk told me you rode in yesterday and I'm in town looking for riders. You are a range man, aren't you?'

'I've done my share of riding,' retorted Wheeler, making up his mind about something. 'Now let me give you a little advice, Mr Cullen. The next time you wake a man up like you did me just now, don't stand in front of him.'

Cullen considered this. 'You a little jumpy?' he inquired, the interest in his eyes spreading downward over his other features.

'I'm not,' Bob said, 'but the next man might be.'

'What's your name, stranger?'

'Bob Smith.'

Cullen was briefly silent. A hint of hard irony appeared down around his mouth. 'It's as good a name as any,' he said, speaking softly. 'I pay fifty a month and found, Smith.'

Wheeler checked an inclination to walk away. This was twenty dollars a month more than was ordinarily paid range riders. He continued to study Cullen. There was something about this cowman, he told himself, that meant trouble. Something arrogantly dangerous too. He could feel his own hardness rising, leaning into a similar hardness coming out of Cullen.

'I'll think about it,' he said.

Cullen snapped: 'You won't have much time. I'll be leaving Kearney in an hour or so.'

Bob nodded and turned his back. He crossed to where the desk clerk was watching Cullen and his companion and asked if the bath was ready. It was; he passed through a draperied opening, entered a small, square room and began to undress. He did not think again of Cullen until, a long and blissful hour later, he was redressed and back in the lobby. Then the clerk asked if the water was hot enough.

'Just right,' Bob told him. 'I feel like a boiled toad but it's a right good feeling.'

The clerk smiled. 'By the way; Mr Cullen asked me to tell you he'd be across the road at the saloon.'

Bob looked momentarily blank. 'Cullen. Cullen the cowman,' he said; then, more swiftly, 'Tell me something; just who the hell is Mr Cullen?'

'Why; he owns Keystone. He's the biggest cowman in these parts.'

'Yeah. And the richest man between here and the Missouri,' Bob said dryly. 'That's not what I want to know. Tell me what you know about him.'

The clerk spread his hands wide. 'Mr

Cullen,' he intoned with exaggerated respect, 'is the law hereabouts. He—'

'Thanks,' Bob said shortly, cutting across the other man's words. 'That's enough. I don't have to know any more than that.'

He went out into the street, sniffed the roiled, leaden-scented night air and watched the sky a moment. There were a few stars shining directly overhead and far, far off in the west a faint and knife-edged lick of forked lightning struck downward. The storm had by-passed Kearney.

Around him there was movement and talk. There were also riders swinging along the darkened roadway heading into, or out of, town. Their faces were touched here and there with reflected lamplight, giving them the appearance and colouring of Indians.

Across the road several men stood gathered together near the entrance to the Palace of Pleasure. Their occasional laughter ran down the night musically fluted. Bob Wheeler watched them idly while considering Cullen's offer.

It might not be a bad idea to ride for Keystone. It would give him an excuse for lingering in the Kearney country, where he was not known, and it would also supply him with the money he would need until he could safely

16

do what he had ridden this far to accomplish. Too, if Mike Barlow was a native of the Kearney area Keystone's riders would know him; whatever the killer of Mike Barlow had to know he could find out from them.

He moved out through the inky dust of the roadway bound for the Palace. As he stepped up onto the far plankwalk several of those idling riders near the doorway threw him a casual glance. He nodded and passed on. One of the men, in the act of turning away, stiffened the full length of his body, then very slowly swivelled his head to watch Bob Wheeler pass from sight into the saloon. He continued to stare after the spindle-doors swung closed. One of the other riders nudged him.

'Hey, Jack—Pete's got another story.'

The cowboy returned his attention forward. As one of his friends began speaking he appeared on the verge of interrupting. But moments passed and he kept silent. It was a dark night, he reasoned, and besides, a lot of men wore ivory-butted guns and were that same size and build. That couldn't have been Bob Wheeler of the Blockton Plains country of Nebraska 'way up here in Nevada. Funny what a few drinks could do to a man's mind. He concentrated on the joke which was being told and he laughed when the others laughed, but he was bothered by the brief look into a face he thought he had recognised, too, and when the idlers broke up, he entered the saloon.

CHAPTER TWO

Harold Cullen was alone at the bar when Bob Wheeler approached, flagging his head at the bartender.

'Sour mash,' he called, and did not look around at Keystone's owner until Cullen spoke, his face curled up into a confident grin.

'I told Eb you'd be along,' Cullen said.

'Who is Eb?' Wheeler asked, taking up his glass.

'That feller who was with me at the hotel. His name's Eb Cartwright.'

'Your foreman?'

Cullen's grin widened. He wagged his head. 'Naw,' he said contemptuously. 'Eb's my cousin. I keep him around to laugh at. He also keeps my books—takes care of the payroll and things like that.' The smile atrophied. Cullen's sharp eyes lingered on Wheeler's profile a moment, then he spoke again. 'Smith—I got a feeling about you.'

'Go on,' said Bob, putting the emptied glass down very gently and turning to fix a long look on the big cowman.

Cullen balanced something in his mind and finally decided against putting it into words. He shrugged. 'It doesn't matter,' he said carelessly. 'Maybe we can discuss it later.' He caught the barman's attention. 'Two repeats down here.'

'No more for me, Mr Cullen. Where is your outfit, when do we head out, and what will my job be?'

Cullen hung fire over his answer, downed his drink first then shrugged again. He was clearly thinking of something remote from Bob's questions.

'The usual chores, Smith. I've got two crews out on roundup. We'll be making up a drive later on. We'll leave in a little while; as soon as Eb gets back. I sent him down to the livery barn for the horses.'

'Then I'd better go saddle up,' said Bob, drawing up off the bar.

'Naw; I told Eb to fetch your critter too.'

Cullen lifted amused eyes to Bob's face. He saw something there that leavened his twinkle a little, and spread both hands in front of him deprecatingly.

'Nothing to get edgy about,' he said. 'Like I told you, I was confident you'd show up.'

'And if I hadn't?'

'I'd have sent Eb back with your horse. No

harm done, Smith.'

There was, Bob thought, something about this man that roiled a person. It wasn't just his arrogance, his overbearing attitude, it went deeper than that. His thoughts were scattered by the arrival of Eb Cartwright.

'The horses are outside,' said Cartwright, throwing a look at Bob which the latter thought showed disappointment; as though Cartwright had mightily wished his cousin had, for once, made the wrong guess about a man.

Cullen threw a coin on the bar and jerked his head. Bob followed him. Behind them came Eb Cartwright, boyishly uncertain eyes fixed on the back of Wheeler. Near the spindle-doors a lounging cowboy kept his gaze fully upon Bob. When the latter's eyes crossed with this intense scrutiny the cowboy's stare dropped away. Something indefinable, like a warning of some kind, flashed outward along Bob's nerves. He rummaged the rider's face for recognition, found nothing there and passed out into the night behind Harold Cullen. He wondered at his edginess.

They mounted, wheeled northward through the pleasant spring night and no one spoke until Kearney was miles behind them, then Cullen said: 'Eb'll take you out to the roundup crew in the morning, Smith. You're a stranger

21

hereabouts so it's not likely you'll know any of the other hands.' Cullen paused, looking straight at Bob. 'There are advantages to being in a new country among strangers,' he said in quiet conclusion.

Bob gave these words a prolonged study. The last sentence told him what he had to know: Cullen thought he was on the dodge, hiding from the law, and yet he had showed no compunction about hiring him, which was interesting. Normally, working cow outfits had no time for men called Smith who came out of nowhere. There was enough to keep men occupied full time at range chores without borrowing trouble or hiring riders who brought trouble with them. His opinion of Harold Cullen was firming up into something he did not like.

'What brought you to Kearney?' Cullen asked.

'Curiosity,' said Bob brusquely, in a tone which discouraged additional questioning.

Cullen nodded, pushing his glance through the night as far as Bob. 'Good,' he said in a tone equally as brusque. 'You'll be far out on the range. Won't run into many people out there except Keystone riders.'

They arrived at Keystone's headquarters buildings on the sunup side of midnight. Cullen

22

left them immediately, without a backward glance, and disappeared into a low, long adobe house. Eb Cartwright held the reins to his and Cullen's mounts; he seemed uneasy. 'Yonder's the bunkhouse,' he told Bob. 'Breakfast is at five o'clock. After that I'll take you out to the holding grounds. Is that all right?'

'Sure,' said Bob kindly, feeling instinctively sorry for this man he knew nothing about. 'Tell me something, Mr Cartwright: just how big an outfit is the Keystone?'

'Thirty thousand acres. We're standing about in the middle of it, Mr Smith. Uh—to the north there's the desert; south and east is open range.'

'And to the west?'

'Well; to the west we go as far as a squatter town called New Hope.'

This last quickened Bob's interest anew. Squatters, in any cow country, were anathema. He watched Cartwright's face when next he spoke.

'Ever have any trouble with the squatters, Mr Cartwright?'

'Well; you probably know how those things are,' the bookkeeper said, and shifted his feet in the dust. 'We'd better put up the horses and turn in. Five o'clock'll be along pretty early.'

Cartwright moved past leading the horses.

Bob watched him over an interval of stillness before trailing along as far as the barn and corrals. Neither of them spoke again. When Bob was alone, finally, he moved through the night as far as Keystone's home-ranch bunk-house and there thumbed back his hat, made a cigarette and smoked it thoughtfully with a great depth of silence around him.

There was nothing new about trouble between homesteaders—called squatters—and the big open-range cow outfits. But to Bob's mind Harold Cullen was not a man to be even temporarily troubled by this. He seemed rather, to be a person who looked beyond each threat to his empire; to be a man who planned carefully not just his next move, but the move beyond that. He seemed, also, to be a man who wove a web around everyone in his employ—like Eb Cartwright—until Harold Cullen's problems were also the problems of his men. This, Bob thought, he could not permit to happen to him. He was not in the Kearney country to serve power or wealth or scheming ambition; he was there simply to kill the gunman who had shot down an eighteen-year-old boy over a card game back in Nebraska. A lad who had been his brother. Beyond that neither Nevada, the people in it nor Harold Cullen's Keystone cow outfit meant anything to him.

He killed the cigarette and entered the bunkhouse. There were only two lumpy shapes slumbering there although both walls were lined with bunks. He selected a lower, dropped down and kicked off his boots. Everyone else would be out with the working crews, he told himself. These men would be the cook, probably, and some ageing or crippled old rider kept around for home-ranch choring. He eased back on the straw pallet, wiggled his toes, sighed, and slept.

Five o'clock, as Cartwright had said, came unpleasantly early. It was the stumping around of his companions in the bunkhouse which awakened him. He cocked an eye at them. One of the men smiled from a face blasted out of life and eroded with the hair-lines of many years and much weathering.

'Mornin',' the older man said. 'Mr Cullen fetch you back from Kearney with him?'

Bob swung his legs over the edge of the bunk. 'Yep,' he grunted, reaching for his boots.

The other man, larger, fatter, with an equally as old a face but with smoother skin, bent a sceptical gaze downward. He watched Bob tug on his boots. 'You always sleep with your gun on?' he asked garrulously.

Bob's rising head swung sideways. 'You

25

object to that?' he asked, stung by the other man's unfriendly tone.

'Why should I object; it's your gun, ain't it?'

The fat man ran his tongue around inside his mouth, spat into a sandbox near the wood stove and stalked out of the room. Behind him the old cowboy cackled softly.

'Don't mind him,' he told Bob. 'I've known Cal Bern close to ten years an' never have I heard him say a good word to anyone when he first gets up in the morning.'

'Is he the *cosinero?*'

'Yep. Home-ranch cook. Too fat'n ornery to go out with the chuck wagon so Harold keeps him here.' The old man stuck out a scarred, sinewy hand. 'Name's Jeb Arbuckle, mister. Proud to know you.' Sly old eyes studied Wheeler.

Bob pumped the hand and dropped it to arise and stretch. 'Bob Smith,' he grunted, watching the old cowboy's expression from the corner of his eye.

But old Jeb Arbuckle had seen too many "Smiths" ride in and ride out in his day to betray by so much as a flicker of an eyelid, what his thoughts were about this latest "Smith".

'Expect we'd best go wash up and eat,' he said, looking beyond the door where new sunlight was rushing hard over the land. 'Cal don't like to be kept waiting.'

The washstand and roller-towel were under an overhang at the rear of the main house. Arbuckle washed first then leaned loosely upon an upright watching Bob wash and dry. He was still wearing the same genial, careful, shrewd look. Only the eyes had changed; as long as Bob's back was to him they were harder, sharper, more calculating.

Breakfast was swiftly concluded; glowering Cal Bern's bleak attitude in the enormous kitchen-dining-hall precluded talk or even pleasantries. Eb Cartwright joined Bob and Jeb Arbuckle with a nod. He had entered the kitchen from within the house. He ate the least and was waiting outside in the yard when Bob emerged.

'I can't take you over this morning,' he said quickly to Bob. 'But Jeb can.' He cast a birdlike glance at the old rider. 'Get a couple of horses, then take Mr Smith out to the holding grounds. He's to work with the round-up crew.'

Jeb moved away with a crab-like, limping gait. Cartwright's eyes stayed on his retreating form as he spoke again.

'The foreman where you're going is a man called Butch Barlow.'

Bob's breath hung up in his throat. He said nothing.

'He'll line you out.'

Cartwright looked up finally. His face was freshly shaven; more boyish-looking than before. Raw yellow sunlight showed him to be slightly built, too, almost fragile. What mildly surprised Bob was something he had not noticed the night before. Beneath his frock coat Eb Cartwright wore a tied-down, walnut-stocked sixgun; he wore it with the grace of a man who knew how to use it and this, Bob thought, was out of character for so obviously a timid man. Then his thoughts reverted to the roundup crew foreman and he asked a question.

'This Butch Barlow—is he Keystone's range boss?'

'Yes. But at gathering time Mr Cullen has Butch make the cut. He puts someone else in charge of the other range crew. You see, Butch is about the best cowman we have; he makes up the drives.'

'He must have an eye for prime beef,' murmured Bob, seeking to draw Cartwright out.

'He has. Keystone beef brings top dollar. Butch knows the best critters. When he makes up a drive it tops out uniform.'

'Is he an old hand at Keystone?'

'Well; Butch's been here about four years now. He'd been here a short time when I came out to work for Mr Cullen. I'm his cousin.'

'He told me that. You keep the tally for him.'

'And other things too.'

'Is Barlow a local rider?'

Cartwright nodded, then caught sight of Jeb leading forward two saddled horses and kept his gaze on the older man. 'Butch and his brother were raised south of Kearney. Their folks had a little sagebrush spread. When they died the boys hired out. Butch's brother, though, he's restless; doesn't stay in one place very long. In fact I heard last night he'd just come back to Nevada after spending about a year down in Nebraska somewhere.'

'Is he a good cowman too?'

Cartwright's smooth face showed a very faint frown. 'No; he's a pretty good rider, but he's not the cowman Butch is. In fact the brother hangs around the towns more than the ranches.' Cartwright squinted into the growing sunlight. 'The brother's name is Mike; he rode for Keystone once, about three years ago, but we let him go. Drank too much and was never around when we needed him.' Cartwright turned, throwing a long look at Bob. 'He hung out over at New Hope, too, and Mr Cullen didn't like that at all.'

'Yeah,' said Bob dryly, and moved out to intercept Arbuckle. 'Well; *adios*.'

'*Adios*,' echoed Cartwright, and stood there

29

in the flashing brightness watching Bob and Jeb Arbuckle ride out across the yard. When they were growing small against the huge, hurting brightness of empty range, Eb turned slightly and called out:

'Jack? Did you get a good look at him?'

From within the big adobe house a man's muted voice preceded him out into the yard. 'Good enough, Eb. Like I told you an' Mr Cullen—it's him all right.'

The rider walked out to stand beside Cartwright in the sunsmash. He, too, stared after the fading horsemen.

'Bob Wheeler of the Blockton country of Nebraska, Eb. Known down there as the fastest gun on the prairies.'

Without taking his eyes off the far-away riders Cartwright said, 'Did Mr Cullen pay you?'

'Yes, sir, he did.'

'Then you'd best ride on,' said Cartwright in a thin and deadly tone which would have surprised Bob Wheeler. 'If we need you we'll send for you down in Kearney.'

The cowboy called Jack started across the yard towards the corrals without another word and Eb Cartwright walked thoughtfully back into the house. There, big Harold Cullen watched him briefly, then drained the coffee cup he was holding and put it down.

'Well,' he said, emphatically, and added nothing to it.

Cartwright tossed his hat aside, ran fingers through his hair and said, 'You didn't have to hire him.'

'No, of course I didn't,' retorted Cullen, looking down upon the slighter man. 'But I'm glad I did. I got no idea what he's up to but I like the idea of having him where we can keep an eye on him, rather than running loose where we can't.'

'Those squatters probably sent for him.'

But Harold Cullen didn't think so. 'Naw,' he snorted. 'You didn't study him very good, Eb. He's not the kind that peddles his gun.'

Cartwright looked squarely into the larger man's face. There was none of the diffidence in his cold expression that Bob had seen, and when next he spoke his voice cracked like a whiplash.

'You've made two mistakes lately, Harold. You'd better not make a third one with this Wheeler feller!'

CHAPTER THREE

From habit Jeb Arbuckle rode through the blasting heat at a leisurely gait. Around both he and Bob Wheeler arid dust boiled up to hang motionless in their wake, its suffocating scent mantling them both with a fine whiteness. After a time the older man said, 'You know a feller named Jack Moffitt?'

Bob said that he did not.

'Funny; when I went to get our horses I seen Jack's critter in the barn. He was sweaty.'

Arbuckle turned a searching glance upon Bob. The younger man returned it in silence. Arbuckle pursed his lips and blew out a breath.

'Jack must've ridden in before sunup. Now that ain't at all like him. He rides sometimes but mostly he hangs around Kearney an' the saloons. Sort of a drifter, too; here for a spell then somewhere else for a spell.'

'What made you think I'd know him?'

'Two things,' replied Jeb. 'One; he shows up the same time you do. Two; he ain't been on Keystone in a year—then all at once here he is. Only...'

'Only what?'

'Where was he? I didn't see hide nor hair of him but there was his horse in the barn an' fresh ridden too.'

Jeb's puzzlement reached Bob. He squinted ahead trying to place the name Jack Moffitt. When he could not he asked Jeb to describe him.

' 'Bout your size, I'd say,' drawled the old cowboy. 'Not so hefty in the shoulders an' arms. 'Bout your age, too; got sort of sandy hair and blue eyes; got a cleft chin an' walks sort of pigeon-toed-like.'

Bob smiled. 'You've just described two-thirds of the range men between here and St Joe,' he said. 'Forget it, Jeb; I don't know him. Besides; just because he rode up about when I showed up doesn't mean anything. Maybe he's got business with Cullen or Cartwright.'

' 'Twouldn't be *good* business,' old Arbuckle murmured under his breath. 'Not if Jack Moffitt's mixed up in it.'

They made the holding grounds shortly before mid-day, but long before they reached them the sound of lowing cattle and the ever-present dust-banner showed that they were getting close.

There was an old mortar trough and a faggot corral; beyond that the only permanent structure at the holding grounds was a thatched ramada under which stood a chuck wagon.

Two grazing herds separated by perhaps three hundred yards of churned, alkaline earth, were being held loosely in check by bored riders. The sky was overcast with heat haze; it hung there as though it was diluted smoke from a forest fire.

As Bob and Jeb stepped off and waited, a short and massively dark man looked out from beneath his hatbrim at them. He was on foot talking to another rider. Both men's shirts were darkly dank with strong sweat. Then the dark man started forward keeping his black stare on Bob.

'New man?' he called to Jeb. The old rider nodded, gazing professionally ahead where the cattle were being cut and sorted.

'Pretty big cut you're making, Butch,' Jeb opined when the range boss stopped close by. 'You culling, too? 'Some cows in the gather born 'bout the same year I was.'

Barlow snorted. 'Hasn't been a cow alive that was born the same year you was, Jeb, in fifty years.' The black stare swung back to Bob. 'I'm Butch Barlow—Keystone range boss.'

'Bob Smith,' said Wheeler, nodding and waiting. 'Mr Cullen hired me last night in Kearney.'

Barlow, Bob thought, did not look at all like his brother. He was shorter, heavier, darker, and from the fullness of his direct stare—tougher. He could be a very dangerous man, and this, concluded Bob, complicated things considerably.

'All right, Smith' the Keystone range boss barked. 'Let's see how good you are. Go find me a fat four-year-old steer in the gather, cut him out and put him yonder with the drive.'

Bob stepped across his mount, a little stung by Butch Barlow's shortness. As he eased forward he glanced down.

'Any particular shade of red you'd like?' he drawled.

Barlow's black gaze brightened but he said nothing. Jeb, however, slapped his thigh and cackled, then he leaned down and said, 'Butch; Cullen figures he's a right good judge of men. Usually he ain't—but this time I think he brought you just about all the man you'll want to fool with.'

Barlow, still watching Bob, said, 'Jeb; you old fool; someday you're going to open your mouth and give your opinion at the wrong time.'

Arbuckle straightened up in the saddle. For just a second his habitual geniality parted to show something less ingratiatingly friendly and

35

diffident, then his fixed expression returned, settled into place and he was again what he appeared always to be: an old rider living out his sundown years in the only element on earth he understood or cared to understand.

Bob eased into the herd riding on a loose rein. He made no hurried move and the cattle, eyeing him askance, were not agitated by his slow-pacing progress. He found the critter he sought—a dark red straight-backed wicked-horned four-year-old with grease enough under his hide to make a bushel of candles, and began working him slowly toward the gather's outer edge. When the steer finally understood that he was being eased away he swung, planting his legs wide and rattling his horns. Bob took down his lariat, flicked the turk's-head end of it, stung the animal's sensitive nose and made a lunge at him. The steer spun away, popped out of the herd and before he could cut back Bob's mount was on him, ears back and teeth bared. In panic the steer fled towards the waiting riders of the drive-herd and was quickly absorbed into that herd.

Bob rode back to Barlow and Jeb Arbuckle, stepped off and returned the shorter, heavier, darker man's gaze. 'Where'll I put my bed-roll?' he asked, thinking privately that the best way to live with a man like Butch Barlow was to give him no trouble and take no trouble from him.

'Under the chuck wagon,' replied the range boss, then walked away.

Bob waited a moment before speaking again, then he thanked Jeb for guiding him to the holding grounds.

' 'Twasn't nothing, young feller.' Arbuckle's eyes were thinned down and drawn out, not altogether from the lemon-yellow sunsmash either; he was watching Butch Barlow's back. 'Do you get sore easy, Mr Smith?' he asked suddenly.

'Not very easy. Why?'

'If I was to offer you a mite of advice would you likely figure an old feller like me's got no call to sound off?'

'No. I'd likely thank him. Never was a man couldn't learn from listening, Jeb.'

Arbuckle continued to gaze outward, his slitted gaze holding steadily ahead. When next he spoke his voice was a notch lower.

'You're a savvy feller; I seen that as soon as I lay my eyes on you. You know enough to keep your eyes open an' your mouth closed. Well; add something else to that: Do what Butch tells you, Mr Smith, an' don't think that because he looks mean that he ain't. Butch Barlow's not just Keystone's top cowman—

he's Keystone's chief gunhand too.'

'I'll remember,' Bob murmured.

Jeb finally looked around and down. Gathering his reins he said, 'I hope you do, Mr Smith. You see, I got a feelin'.'

'Yeah?'

'Yeah. You didn't hire out to Keystone just because you like to sweat.' He turned his horse. 'It ain't none of my affair an' I ain't going to make it so either. But you just remember what I said—don't mix with Butch Barlow, and whatever you got in mind, you just might live long enough to do. Otherwise—no.'

Bob watched the old rider move off; was still staring after him when Keystone's range boss bellowed his name.

'Get astride, Smith. Another gather's coming. He'p the boys push these other critters back a mile or two.'

The routine of making up a drive-herd did not vary. One range crew gathered a herd and drove it to the holding grounds. There the experienced cutting-riders selected the primest animals under Butch Barlow's supervision, cut them out and drove them to the drive-herd which was being held apart by more riders. When the prime animals had all been cut out, the gather was drifted out on the range again and other riders brought in another gather.

It was not particularly hard work, but it was hot, dusty, monotonous and often dangerous work. Range-critters who only saw horsemen once or twice a year for four years—before they were cut out and put into the drive-herd—and who had spent those four years fighting among themselves, fighting wolves, cougars and sometimes bears, were not amenable to human direction; they were as likely to charge one way as the other. Many a crippled cowboy spent his later years cursing cat-footed big-horned range critters—and a horse which more often than not died gutted because he was not quick enough to shy away in time.

Bob Wheeler was as good as any of Butch Barlow's other riders and he was better than most of them. He could, in fact, cut out prime beef without Barlow's supervision and while he and Barlow remained a trifle stiff towards one another the range boss never questioned his choices.

After sundown the *remuderos*—riders who watched over the saddle-stock herd—went with the horses to a distant bedding ground where they had a separate camp, and the balance of the riders ate supper squatting near the chuck wagon. It was here Bob got to know the men of Keystone's cutting crew; eight of them, Harold Cullen's top hands. They were in many ways alike; careful with their words, good listeners, unrestrained in their humour; men with untold dreams and secret pasts. Single men, mostly, and three of them were Mormons. Typical range men; they could have been wanted in five Western states or they could have been choir singers, it was impossible to tell which from their looks, their language, or their reluctance to speak of themselves. There was not a coward among them, and if they had never killed another man it did not mean that they wouldn't.

Where Bob had trouble was in placing them in some scheme he was convinced Harold Cullen was involved in. None of them had the look of gunfighters, but again, there was no way to tell. Even without Jeb Arbuckle's warning about the range boss he would have considered him a handy man with a gun; but the others appeared to him no different from dozens of riders he'd known from the Flint Hills to Mexico and back again. But he also knew that a cattleman could become a gunman simply by changing the direction he was facing; it took practice but these men had the time for it in the dreary winters, in the long lonely days alone upon the range. You never knew which man wearing a gun was the deadliest until, very often, it was too late to correct earlier impressions.

But there was something else, and Bob never once overlooked it. It was the unchanging constant in the lives of range men. Loyalty. As long as a rider took an outfit's pay, rode its horses and pushed his legs under its supper table, he served its interests without qualification, without questioning, and without betraying it.

If a rider did not like what he was called upon to do he saddled up, drew his time, and rode on. But as long as he remained he did what must be done within the law or without it. This was the simple, forthright law of the cow country and men as uncomplicated as Keystone's riders, sat now, in the quickening dusk of a spring evening, smoking, speaking desultorily, gradually and inadvertently painting a picture for Bob Wheeler that clarified many things. It was a rider called simply 'Dusty' who said he had cropped seven pairs of ears that day.

Reno Carson, a Mormon and the best rope-hand of the crew, lit up, exhaled and spoke through bluish-smoke. 'It's beginning to add up,' he said casually. 'Dusty got seven today, I got three yesterday, Turk got eight the day before.' Reno Carson's untroubled gaze went from face to face. 'Goin' to be some pretty fair bonuses paid out after the drive.' The Mormon's eyes twinkled. 'I think I'll take my found-money down to San Francisco and get into one of them high-falutin' faro games they got down there.'

'You'll lose your hide,' the range boss told Carson. ' 'Cause a man's good with rope don't make him good with playin' cards.'

But Reno Carson had rationalised about this and had his answer ready. 'If I lose, what have I lost? Bonus money isn't like wages. It's like finding money. Found-money I call it.'

'It's still money,' Barlow mumbled. 'And another thing; it ain't going to take those squatters long to figure out what's happening to their critters, either. When they quit ear-marking and start branding that'll be the end of our found-money.'

A lanky, hawk-faced thin man called 'Turk', spoke now, his body lying out full length upon the ground, his steady gaze upon the earth's distant curve. 'By the time they find out there won't be much left for 'em to brand,' he said. After a thoughtful moment he said more. 'Mr Cullen an' Mr Cartwright got the right idea. I've seen range wars in my time an' I can tell you for a fact don't neither side win 'em. This beats gunnin' them and burnin' them out four ways from the middle. Like Mr Cullen says— break 'em financially. You don't have to kill 'em and spend the rest of your days hidin' from the law—just bankrupt 'em.'

Bob lowered his head to concentrate upon the cigarette he was twisting up. It was clear to him now why Cullen would hire a man he thought might be an outlaw. It was also clear what Cullen was involved in. He inhaled, exhaled, and turned an even gaze upon the range boss.

'You mind telling me what this is all about?' he asked.

Barlow's complete attention turned upon him. 'No, I don't mind, Smith,' he said. 'Every man in the cuttin' crew gets a two-dollar bonus for every squatter-critter he turns into the drive-herd.'

Bob nodded comprehension. 'The squatters don't brand, I take it.'

'They only earmark. Some on one ear, some on both ears.' Barlow's dark gaze sparkled. 'If you find a critter that isn't branded but has an earmark, you rope him, cut off both ears, push him into the drive-herd and fetch the ears to me. I keep a tally-book an' when the drive-herd is all made up I turn the book in to Mr Cullen an' he pays you the two-dollar bonus.'

Eight pairs of unmoving eyes lingered on the new rider. Smoke curled upwards around hat-brims and unreadable faces shone fitfully in the curling light of the cook-fire.

'That,' said Bob finally, 'takes some of the

43

drudgery out of this sweating.'

Slowly, smiles came and approving eyes dropped away. Reno Carson broke the ensuing silence. 'It sure does,' he agreed.

CHAPTER FOUR

The following day, his sixth at Keystone, Bob Wheeler cut out and docked the ears off four critters. Butch Barlow duly recorded that he had earned eight dollars in bonus money that day. The seventh day, a Saturday, he found no squatter-critters, and the eighth day, Sunday, everyone but a skeleton crew saddled up before dawn and lit out for the home ranch, their wages, and the afterward long ride into Kearney.

It was subsequent to their arrival at the home ranch, where the range boss had gone at once to the main house, that Bob noticed a difference in Barlow. On the ride to Kearney he caught Butch watching him twice, both times secretly, from beneath a tugged-forward hat-brim, and each time, before the range boss looked away, Bob had seen fire-points of distrust and antagonism in Barlow's gaze.

Something had been said back at the ranch, Bob now thought, which had turned Barlow fully against him. This caused him less concern than the knowledge that Cullen either knew

45

something about him or suspected something, which now put his life in peril. These men did not play games.

The afternoon was half gone and the heat had reached its compounded intensity by the time Keystone's cutting crew loped up over the curve of the plain bearing swiftly down upon Kearney. Nothing relieved that heat; there were no trees; no shadow-high brush of any kind. Riding was punishment, each breath a labour; the surfeiting thought of Kearney's shade, its saloons and strong coolness encouraged the men to pass swiftly onward until they cut into Kearney's north-south yellow streak of a stage road. With each ugly outline of the town clearly visible in that heat-hazed powdery world the men dropped down to a slamming trot and kept steadily to it without speaking until they came down in a moving body to Kearney's north environs; then they slowed to a loose walk as far as the livery barn and there swung off.

'Corral 'em,' Butch called shortly to an advancing hostler. 'Keystone horses to themselves.'

The men scattered and Bob, watching the range boss, saw Barlow hesitate, torn between a desire to follow after towards the Palace, or do something which he clearly felt was both an

46

obligation and an intrusion on his free time. Finally though, Barlow split off heading purposefully towards the sheriff's office.

Bob was piqued. He hung back and after the last Keystone rider had faded beyond the Palace's spindle-doors, he crossed through the burnished dust to where an earthen olla hung suspended beneath the overhang of a general store, slapped dust from his shirt, spat cotton, upended the olla and drank all he could hold, unable to slake the thirst that was in him.

He afterwards sought a shaded bench, sank down there, thrust his legs forth to their full length and from time to time threw an outward, long gaze towards the sheriff's office.

It was not a long vigil, but after Butch Barlow reappeared on the plankwalk striding hurriedly towards the Palace, Bob kept his vigil. He had a small piece of something.

A man left the sheriff's office, crossed to the telegrapher's cubbyhole and entered. He was lost to Bob's gaze for no more than ten minutes, then emerged into the sun-glare and plodded back the way he had come.

The events Bob had seen began to firm up in his mind into a kind of sequence. Cullen had evidently told Barlow something about their new rider; had perhaps sent Barlow to Kearney's sheriff, and the sheriff had then wired someone to verify something.

But what? Bob was not a wanted man. Nor did he think it would have caused Harold Cullen or Butch Barlow much concern if he had been. Then what was happening?

He arose, a tall, sinewy man burnt brown, and stretched to his full height making the shadow behind him grow enormously, curving upwards from the bench along the back wall.

A man in a town where other men could become his enemies at no more than the drop of a word, the hardening of a steady gaze, or the blur of a gun-hand, could afford no mistakes. The answer to this fresh riddle lay in the telegrapher's office but by now there would be suspicious eyes following him. He could not approach the telegrapher as long as daylight held.

He turned to scrutinise the store-fronts around him. There was a café close by. He headed for that, not hungry but needing privacy at least for a while, needing solace for the length of time it would take to fit a number of random thoughts into some sort of order.

An hour later, squared around at the café counter staring outward upon Kearney's broad thoroughfare, studying the faces which passed and the lengthening shadows too, he came face to face with the only decision he had; the identical decision he had confronted nearly two weeks earlier when he had stood back in the dark of a storm-torn night waiting to kill a man.

He could saddle up right now, this night, and ride out. Or he could stay, and although he might yet kill Mike Barlow, other men would also die and he might very easily be among them. Beyond the window sunlight blazed in a last great burst of flame, then the red gorge of it was gone, sucked mysteriously beyond that farspending rind of earth to explode in another world, and dusk came up out of the earth to soften lines, ameliorate harshness, tame the galling heat and quell that leaching aridity.

He would stay.

Three men came from the Palace across the way, stood motionless upon the plankwalk's edge for a moment, then stepped down into the roadway dust and moved together upon the hotel. They had a purpose and a destination, Bob thought, watching them until the warped plane of near-side buildings sliced them from view, and one of them had been Butch Barlow.

He stood up, tossed a coin upon the counter to pay for his pie and coffee, and moved forward. A fourth man left the saloon, his body alternately clear and blurred as dripping darkness fell over him. He was tall, hawkish, and wore the hard-brimmed Stetson of the Keystone rider called Turk. He would have moved off after the other three but a looming silhouette called forth, stopping him. Bob could see the little star on the newcomer's shirt, and he could hear his words plainly.

'Where's Butch?'

'I don't know,' lied Turk, obviously leery now. 'Why?'

'I got an answer to the telegram I sent for him.'

'Oh. You might try the hotel. I think he might be over there. I don't know for sure though.'

The sheriff's sharp-boned shoulders swung outward moving into the roadway, Bob watched him until Turk swung back into the saloon, then he too moved, but more swiftly than either the lawman or the Keystone rider.

The sheriff was veering off to enter the hotel when a hurrying tall cowboy lunged forward striking him hard, nearly upsetting him. Strong hands caught at his shirt supporting him while a hatbrim-shadowed face spoke quick and throaty apologies. Then the rider was hastening on past. The sheriff swore and ran a hand under his handlebar moustache and swore some more, but the unknown rider was gone in the night.

In the reflected back alley light of the café

Bob smoothed out the telegram's yellowish paper and held it close. 'Man you wired about is not wanted in this territory,' the message read. 'He is not an outlaw.' There was a signature: 'Sheriff Tim Beasley, Brockton, Nebraska.'

Bob brought his squinted eyelids closer together in a slow, mirthless smile. Tim Beasley had reason to aid him but that was not, at this moment, a thing to rejoice over.

He let enough time elapse to feel safe, then went sauntering down the plankwalk in front of the hotel, dropped the telegram and continued onward as far as the lamplit window of Kearney's solitary saddle and harness shop, and there faded back into darkness watching and wondering.

What had prompted Cullen to send that message? It was not, Bob felt convinced, that he objected to having outlaws in Keystone's employ. Then why? That Cullen knew who he was intrigued him; and after some additional thought he came to the conclusion that if Cullen knew, Butch Barlow also knew, and it must therefore be only a short wait before Butch's brother also knew. And when Mike Barlow heard the name Bob Wheeler—they would all know why he was in Nevada.

Beyond that, unless he was able to influence

events, it required no great foresight to imagine what lay ahead.

One thing was quite clear; he could not return to Keystone. This made him smile. Cullen's range boss would very shortly now, haul up short with the realisation that Bob Wheeler knew Keystone's plan to ruin the squatters. Between Barlow, Cullen, and perhaps Cartwright too, they would take every desperate means they could devise to kill him; they had to; and most deadly among his new adversaries was Butch Barlow, who now had two reasons to want Bob Wheeler dead.

He made a slow-swinging search of the night and saw, northward in the roadway, a group of heatedly arguing men in front of the hotel. One man there, clutching a yellow slip of paper in his fist, was vehemently speaking. He was short and square-hewn in the night, and Bob had no difficulty imagining what his expression was like. Butch Barlow had also put some loose ends together.

He wheeled clear of the saddle shop window and made for a dog-trot between two buildings. There, shoulders brushing rough adobe on both sides, he made his way into a littered backlot. He could not return for his horse and very shortly now Keystone, and Keystone's friends in Kearney, would be plumbing the night for him. The ways of violence, he thought, were never changing, never different, and they were at this moment beginning to uncoil in this ugly little desert town.

Beyond the commonplace sounds of Kearney came now the heavy-slamming urgency of a horseman heading northward in a straining run. Going for Cullen, he told himself. Cullen and perhaps his fragile shadow, Eb Cartwright. He had to keep moving; Barlow's remaining men would by now be scattering out, searching, moving swiftly through the night probably with the incentive of another kind of bonus urging them on.

He crossed hurriedly over the backlot into a wealth of dark gloom near an unkempt old church with an askew, thin wooden cross atop its domed peak. Here, pausing briefly for breath and bearings, he sighted the vague silhouette of a saddled horse. Not until he was reaching for the looped reins did he notice the Kentucky spring-seat side-saddle with which the docile beast was cinched up. And in that precise same second came an unmistakable sharp snippet of sound, which anyone, once having heard, never again forgets; the cocking of a gun. He remained wholly motionless.

'Take your hand off those reins!'

He drew away his arm and remained stone-like.

'Turn around!'

Obedience was a natural thing under these circumstances but what came next was much less than he had expected. The unwavering gunbarrel's solitary dark eye was fixed permanently upon his belt buckle. The hand aiming it was firm and quite small. Behind the hand was a girl. Where silvery starshine lay across her face it showed with pale integrity the smoothness of firm flesh and the regularity of good features. She was a very lovely thing to gaze upon even with the gun between them.

'I wasn't going to steal him,' said Bob, telling half the truth.

The girl supplied the other half in a dry voice. 'Not after you saw my side-saddle. Who are you?'

'My name is Wheeler. Until this evening I worked for Cullen's Keystone outfit.'

'I can believe that,' the handsome girl said in that same dry tone, leaving no doubt about her opinion of Keystone and its men. 'When Keystone fires a man he's so bad even the renegades won't associate with him.'

'Lady; Keystone didn't fire me.'

'Oh,' that dry voice said, warming the

smallest bit with curiosity. 'You must have a conscience then—but you were still going to steal my horse.'

'Lady,' Bob said, letting some of his stiffness dwindle. 'I don't have time to explain. Can I go now?'

'Why should I let you go; so you can steal someone else's horse?'

'Ma'am; do you know who Butch Barlow is?'

'Certainly.'

'He and his crew are hunting for me right this minute. I can't go back to the livery barn and get my horse.'

'So you would have stolen mine.'

'Lady,' said Bob in growing desperation, 'I am not a horsethief—but—'

'Why is Keystone after you?'

'Lady, please—point that thing some other way. I don't have time to explain.'

He teetered forward. The pistol barrel tilted and remained sightlessly staring.

'Walk up those steps,' the girl said. 'Go through that side door into the chapel. When he frowned, gazing past at the dark and gloomy old church front, the pistol flagged at him. 'Hurry up; there is someone coming.'

He went forward and passed hurriedly into a silence deeper than the night. Two pale candles burnt beyond, in the little room, and as he turned, the girl eased closed a huge and age-blackened oaken door. She lowered the gun.

'Now tell me,' she ordered. 'This is the last place in the world a Keystone rider would look for another Keystoner.'

Beyond in the night he heard a bull-bass voice roar impatiently with the force of a hammer striking iron: 'Damn you, *find him!*' He moved up near the girl listening at the door. Outside there was the sound of several men moving hurriedly, their spurs making it possible for the listening man and girl to assess their progress.

'He ain't back here,' a breathless voice called irritably. 'We're wasting time. He'll be 'round front tryin' to get a horse.'

'Come on then,' Butch Barlow snarled. 'He can't get far.'

The girl at his side said, 'They're going away.'

Bob looked down into her face on the verge of agreeing when he heard, just beyond the door, soft-grinding boot-leather. He put a finger to his lips for silence and faced away. The latch began to rise. Perhaps the man outside had heard the girl speak. Possibly not. At any rate he pushed inward with his gun-hand extended.

When candlelight struck gently against blue steel Bob moved. He caught at the man's wrist jerking him bodily into the room. The Keystone man gasped, struggled to right himself, and half turned. Bob hooked a chopping punch upwards from his belt into the cowboy's jaw and drove him back in a spinning stagger. He felled him with the second blow and stood over him listening. Beyond the door the night was silent.

'Who is he?' asked the girl, hands clasped together and her eyes wide.

'His name's Reno Carson,' replied Wheeler. 'He's one of Butch Barlow's cutting crew.'

When he faced around the girl was watching him with a direct and speculative expression on her face. Even as he held her gaze with his own, which was smoky now from the excitement of combat, he saw her mouth change; her lips form a new expression; softer, more feminine.

'I'd better leave you now,' he told her. 'They won't quit looking until they find me, and they'll miss Carson sooner or later. If you're with me you might get hurt.'

'I have a better plan,' said she. 'Obviously you don't know this town very well. I do. I'll take you where they'll never find you.'

'You're buying into something that isn't a

woman's game, lady,' he said a little impatiently.

She responded to the urgency in his voice by
reaching for the door latch. 'We can talk later.
I'll walk out to my horse. When I'm satisfied
it's safe for you to follow me I'll mount, then
circle my horse. When you see me do that
you come out and follow me. But stay in the
shadows where you can.' She partially opened
the door looking into his eyes. 'All right, Mr
Wheeler?'

'All right, Miss...'

'Miss McDonald. Aimee McDonald.'

CHAPTER FIVE

As Aimee McDonald had implied, she knew Kearney better than Bob Wheeler did. She led him by a circuitous, back-alley route, to the dilapidated horse-shed of a large home at the extreme west end of town. There, while he stood in full darkness, she off-saddled, forked hay to her mount, smoothed her dress and came back into the point of vigil where he stood looking out into the yonder night.

'No one saw us, Mr Wheeler.'

He ignored her to continue his taking of the pulse of this deadly night. She put up a hand, touched his chest and pushed him back away from the door.

'Close the door. It's always kept closed. Anyone looking this way will notice that it's open.'

When he did not move at once to obey she pushed the door closed herself then faced around towards him. It was quite dark in the horse-shed now, but a late-rising Comanche moon, tilted upwards, silvered the yard beyond and passed into the shed where the old boards were cracked and warped. It touched them both a little, gently emphasising the difference between them. Her head scarcely came up to his shoulder and where he had squint-lines around his eyes she had none.

He looked down at her lips. They lay gently closed, full at the centres and softly curving. When he moved his gaze slightly he found her large eyes were fully upon him with an expression which gradually became veiled and heavy.

'I think you must be adventuresome,' he told her. 'Maybe you should have been a boy.'

She smiled upwards. 'My father has always said that. Now tell me why they are after you.'

He did not wish to tell her he had come to Kearney expressly to kill a man, but in his hesitant reaching for a different approach he found no other way to begin, so he told her, speaking bluntly as he might have done with another man, precisely what his trouble now was.

She listened in long silence never once lowering her eyes, and when he finished she continued quiet for a moment longer, then murmured: 'You must be very careful. Keystone has many friends.'

'It must also have enemies,' he stated.

'It has; mostly among the settlers over near New Hope.'

'Not around Kearney?'

She shrugged, studying him again. 'It has enemies here, Mr Wheeler, but not many.' She considered his ivory-stocked pistol and the way it was lashed to his leg, for a thoughtful moment, then raised her head.

'This is a man's country, Mr Wheeler, and the men here are mostly cattlemen—owners or riders. They respect wealth and power like men do everywhere, and hereabouts Keystone has the most money and the most influence.'

'Even the law, I understand,' he said wryly, 'belongs to Keystone.'

At this she rummaged his face for more meaning, then, finding nothing more she slowly murmured: 'No; not the law. It may appear that way to a stranger, Mr Wheeler, but Keystone doesn't own the law.'

'You know that for a fact, Miss McDonald?'

She faintly smiled. 'I was born here. I've lived here all my life. No; Keystone doesn't own the law.'

She drew up off the door, removed her little hat and brushed away a red-iron wisp of a curl from her forehead. Their eyes met in a final long look and he saw want come to her. Without speaking or scarcely moving he reached downward and outward, touched her waist and swayed her up against him. He kissed her full on the lips with a heavy gentleness, then stepped back.

Her forthright gaze was blacker now and unfathomable. She might not have felt the rough edge of his hunger at all in that kiss, for she now said, simply: 'Mr Wheeler; if you wait here until an hour or two before sunup, then leave, I don't think you'll be in much danger.'

She turned, reaching for the door. He caught her arm, half turning her. 'I apologise,' he said roughly.

She looked sideways up into his face, saying gravely, 'You don't have to. I'm not sorry you did that.' She opened the door. 'We'll meet again, Mr Wheeler,' she murmured, then was gone.

It took a while for his roiled pulse to run back down to normal and when it did, finally, he touched his lips remembering. And he also wondered at that drive in a man which drove him to kiss a beautiful girl at a time when a bullet might come out of the night at any moment and kill him. It had to be a very powerful impulse, he reasoned, within a man, to make him deliberately turn his back upon death to kiss a woman.

He smoked and thought and waited out the small hours, then he left the horse-shed, circled the town stealthily, came down behind the livery barn, found an unexpected Keystone horse in the public corrals looped up a war-bridle from a tie-rope, got onto the beast and struck out westerly for the squatter town of New Hope.

No living man could fight Keystone alone; not even the fastest gun in Nebraska—or *from* Nebraska. He would first secure help, then he would return.

But during that long westerly ride he had troubled thoughts, too, for he had not come to Nevada to beard a cow outfit; only to kill one man. It rankled, of course, that Keystone had made him a fugitive, but he asked himself if it rankled enough for him to accept the over-whelming odds he must face in a show-down fight with the Keystone cow outfit.

He did not at once arrive at a decision about this because the memory of that kiss in the horse-shed diverted his thoughts again and again; until New Hope was fully in sight ahead of him in the quickening, fresh and fragrant dawn.

The pull of Aimee McDonald's presence had been difficult to resist from that moment when she had first faced him with a cocked gun be-tween them. Never before in his life had a woman affected him like that. Just gazing at her had made him strain against the propriety which was a large part of his upbringing. His

63

mind kept reverting to this. And in the end he had succumbed; had kissed her mouth, for whether Aimee willed it or not she pulled a man, drew him against even his own wishes.

'...We will meet again, Mr Wheeler.'

He halted the Keystone horse a half mile from New Hope studying the dawn-greyed buildings ahead. Yes, he said to himself, they would meet again. And in that sentence he found the answer to his other question; the question of fighting Keystone. He would have to fight Cullen, Cartwright, the Barlow brothers and anyone else who opposed him, because if he left Nevada now he and Aimee would *not* meet again, and if he stayed so that they might meet again, Keystone would be on hand to try for his life. He kneed the horse forward and entered New Hope from the east, riding forward as far as a newly-erected slab building which was the livery stable, his decision fully made.

The sheriff of New Hope was a grizzled, ham-handed man with suspicious eyes and a tough-set mouth. He said nothing when Bob entered his office and continued to sip steaming coffee from a tin mug.

'Get yourself a cup,' he said shortly. 'There's more in the pot on the stove.'

Bob helped himself, returned to the table

where the sheriff sat and gazed wonderingly at the older man. 'My name's Bob Wheeler,' he said, and waited.

'Mine's Charley Crowninshield. I watched you ride in, cowboy.' Crowninshield sipped, sighed and settled back. 'On that Keystone horse,' he added with a significant stare. 'A little west of your stamping grounds, aren't you? I mean; Keystoners aren't real welcome over here, you know.'

Bob's tiredness diminished under the stimulus of that strong black coffee. He put the cup aside to make a cigarette. 'I didn't come here to run for mayor,' he said, lighting up and exhaling. 'I came here to ask if you people have been losing cattle.'

Sheriff Crowninshield's steady gaze brightened; turned sharp and appraising. 'We have,' he stated. 'That's no secret.'

'Quite a few lately?'

'Within the past five days it's been estimated that we've lost over three hundred head.'

'Any ideas, Sheriff?'

Crowninshield shifted in his chair. 'Sure. We got ideas, cowboy. Plenty of ideas. The hell of it is you got to have more'n suspicions to make arrests.'

Crowninshield pushed the tin mug away from him and bent a long stare upon Bob. The latter could see Crowninshield's spirit harden against him in spite of the man's curiosity. He ignored this to ask a question.

'I was told last night that the law around here doesn't belong to Keystone. I thought it did. What do you think?'

'What of it?'

'Could you get the law at Kearney to cooperate with you in prosecuting Keystone for rustling squatter beef?'

Sheriff Crowninshield's sunk-set eyes kindled with testiness. 'If I could make a case, mister, by God I'd sure try,' he growled. 'Now let's quit playin' games. I watched you ride in an' I expect by now everyone for a half mile in every direction knows there's a Keystone range rider in my office.' Crowninshield's squared jaw held briefly closed before he resumed speaking. 'Young feller—by the way you pack that gun I know you're good at using it—but let me tell you this, too: For the past week now I've had from three to ten complaints every single damned day about settler-beef disappearing. I couldn't keep these folks from lynching a Keystoner now if I wanted to—and I'm not sure I want to. So, like I said, let's quit playing games. You got something on your mind, or did you ride over here show how brave Keystoners are?'

66

'I can tell you how your beef is rustled.'

'I don't doubt that,' the sheriff replied. 'The question is—*will* you tell me?'

'Yes.'

Crowninshield drummed softly on the table-top. 'Why?' he asked finally. 'You know what Cullen an' Cartwright'll do to you for helping settlers, mister?'

'I have an idea. They tried to do it last night, and I hadn't even talked to a squatter then.'

Crowninshield continued to drum on the table. Eventually he said, 'I think I'm beginning to understand. All right then, stranger; sit down an' let's clear the air with a little straight talk.'

Bob sat. He dropped the cigarette from his hand and decapitated it with one roll of a spur rowel, then he told Sheriff Crowninshield in short sentences how the Keystone riders earned their bonuses at the holding grounds. He even told him that he, himself, had docked four pairs of ears.

'If your people used hot irons instead of pocket knives,' he said in conclusion, 'that would be the end of it.'

'They're using irons,' the sheriff told him. 'But they only just started it.' He leaned forward in the chair. 'They're ridin', too, but they can't trespass on Keystone. I told 'em that. Of course they're trespassin' anyway, but the trouble with that is I can't lift a hand to help them if they get into trouble over doing it.' Crowninshield muttered a coarse word then fixed his uncompromising stare upon Bob again. 'I'd like you for a deputy,' he said, 'but I think first we've got to get the folks hereabouts to accept you.'

'I've worn a badge before,' said Bob succinctly. 'Now I'd rather not. I've got a man to kill. I can't do it wearing a badge and I didn't ride all the way to Nevada to be talked out of killing him.'

Crowninshield sat still. He said, 'A Keystoner?'

'Not exactly—but there's a tie-in.'

'That's good enough for me, Mr Wheeler. I don't want to know any more though; in my job I'm not supposed to hold with gunfights.'

Crowninshield arose. He was a sloping-shouldered, physically powerful man with an unrelenting air of forthrightness to him. 'There's no judge here to sign warrants, Mr Wheeler. I'll have to send a man to the county seat.' He looked down. 'You plumb sure you'll appear against those Keystoners that stole settler-beef?'

'Plumb sure,' said Bob, also standing up.

'They'll be after you like the Grim Reaper

68

himself. Your chances will be pretty good of not livin' out the summer. I want you to know that, Mr Wheeler. I want you to cogitate on it too, so's you'll stand by your word to testify—or drop out right here and now—not leave me with a bunch of worthless warrants.'

Bob's reply came firmly. 'I've weighed all this, Sheriff. I'll stand behind my word.'

Crowninshield reached for his hat, crushed it on and swung towards the door. 'I'll send a feller for the warrants.' From the doorway he said: 'Mr Wheeler—have you any idea how many men Eb Cartwright has killed in fair fights?'

Bob's eyes widened. 'Cartwright?' he murmured. 'You mean Butch Barlow, don't you?'

'No, sir. I mean Eb Cartwright.' Sheriff Crowninshield's expression turned sardonic. 'I see you're another newcomer to this country who's been taken in by Cartwright's timid act. Well; forget Barlow. He's handy but he's first of all a cowboy. Eb Cartwright's a professional gunman. He come out here a few years back to help Harold Cullen expand Keystone, and he's done every bit of it with his guns.' Crowninshield began to thinly smile.

'Mr Wheeler; I've seen him draw an' I don't think there's a man living who can beat him.'

When Bob was left alone in Sheriff Crowninshield's office he drew himself a second cup of coffee, went to the doorway and gazed out into New Hope's raw and sun-scorched thoroughfare.

That, he told himself, was how men died. That was *why* they died in the roadway dust of a hundred cow towns looking astonished, looking unbelieving; because you never knew how deadly a man was until you were there facing him.

He drained off the coffee and tapped the cup with his free hand. It made a difference when a person was warned; in his case perhaps it made all the difference, because he never would have turned away from Barlow to watch Cartwright—and that would have been the one mistake he would never live to rectify.

CHAPTER SIX

The word had been passed in New Hope by Sheriff Crowninshield, but on every hand Bob felt the coldness, the veiled yet savage hostility his presence evoked at the café, the hotel, and particularly at the bar. He did not greatly blame the squatters, but being sympathetic did not prevent him from being watchful either. It was this wariness that kept him safe on a hot afternoon when men's tempers, rubbed raw by heat and loss and persecution, brought New Hope's bitterness into the open.

'You there,' a voice said fiercely as he was moving out from the plankwalk. 'You Keystoner!'

He turned, each nerve alerted, every muscle turning ready. The man who had called was about Bob's size, but more solid. Around him were others like him; dressed the same in low-heeled, coarse and functional cowhide boots, floppy hats and nondescript tow-cloth shirts, dark now with sweat. Only two of them wore guns. The man who glared outward did not. His hands were fisted, his shoulders hunched forward.

'When your own kind kicks you out you come whining to us. Ain't nothin' lower'n a yellow range man!'

Bob waited, knowing this compact farmer wished to fight; seeing in his bearing, his attitude, the identical stance and expression he had dozens of times faced in other places. The clod-hopper was bronzed by sunshine; he was also scarred and capable-looking; he had survived much violence and, Bob now thought, probably most of it had been of his own making, for obviously, he was governed by passion.

'You better back off,' said Bob quietly, eyeing the two armed men. 'I don't want to fight you—and I don't like the idea of two guns behind me if I have to.'

The squatter growled a strong oath. 'Never mind *them*,' he said with loud emphasis. 'They won't sit in, cowboy.' He looked briefly at his companions; a thought passed between them. The crowd was growing now, drawn forward by the farmer's loud voice. 'You shuck that gun, Keystoner, and I'll rub your nose in the dust.' The man started flat-footedly forward. 'If you don't shuck it I'll rub your nose in the goddamned dirt anyway.'

There was no alternative for Bob; the squatter was committed and the hunger for combat

72

was a shine in his eyes; it was also cast clearly in the stone-set bulge of his jaw. Bob removed his pistol, rolled the shell-belt and placed it gently off to one side a few feet.

The farmer came on, still speaking strongly, cursing range men, Keystone; calling them killers and cow thieves and much worse. Bob was not fooled; it was an ancient stratagem, this talking to divert an adversary. He rocked slightly forward on the balls of his feet and when the settler swung all the way from his knees and missed, to fall awkwardly into Bob, the Nebraskan was ready. He twisted from the taloned, groping fingers, aimed a short jab and lashed out. The farmer was rocked. He lowered his head to hide his face from another strike and sawed in a big shuddering breath. He was hurt.

Bob was clear. He stood there waiting, not once looking away from the heavier man. Along the plankwalk men, even several slatternly women, were calling encouragement to the farmer and insults to Bob.

Coming on again the settler planted each foot solidly forward. When Bob did not retreat he threw wild blows and bored in. Then Bob made a mistake; he waited too long to punch and dance away. The farmer, anticipating this from what had occurred before, absorbed the blow and sprang sideways also. He instantly collided with the leaner man, bore him backwards to the edge of the plankwalk, where scattering bystanders squealed, and when Bob's spurs caught at the wood and he fell the squatter's weight continued downward too, his body across Wheeler's body, his fingers frantically searching for Bob's eyes and his strong breath pantingly close and offensive.

Instinct made Bob bow his neck, curve his head into the settler's shoulder to protect his face, and at the same time twist to avoid the slamming knee which struck his hip instead of his groin. Then, with both arms, he took a round-about grip on his adversary's belly and began to squeeze. The farmer gasped, he writhed. His soft parts were constricted; each second the pressure increased and the pain and suffocation became more intense. He beat helplessly upwards raining blows upon Bob's back and shoulders. His eyes bulged, his mouth was widely open disclosing its dank inner pinkness. Then Bob sprang, his arms wide and the farmer let out a great gasp and sagged, sucking greedily for air, unmindful of the man who got from beneath him, rolled over to spring up, and caught him a merciless blow with the full weight of a downward-driven bony fist on the back of the neck. The farmer, hanging there on all fours, collapsed with a choked-off grunt and did not move again.

From the small space left to him on the sidewalk Bob leaned into the stares of hatred surrounding him and gulped air into burning lungs. His heart sounded in his ears, louder than a beaten drum. When he was able he retrieved his gun, belted it on, punched his trodden hat back into shape and tugged it on. Not until then did he speak; not until then was he able to speak.

'Listen,' he said to the glowering bystanders, 'I'm in your damned town to help you, not fight you. If I'd wanted to fight you I'd have stayed at the Keystone.'

He turned away, trudged through roadway dust as far as a public watering trough, and there sluiced sweat, dust and grime off, with wet coolness. One of his knuckled hands was raw and slightly hurting. He flexed it; it was not his gun-hand and that was uppermost in his mind.

That same day but later, in the evening, Sheriff Crowninshield's warrants arrived. He showed them to Bob at the New Hope Café, and for a long afterward moment peered out at the younger man with speculation strong in his gaze.

'You haven't changed your mind have you?' he asked.

Bob wagged his head, finished his supper and pushed back. 'No,' he replied. 'I'm ready whenever you are.'

'Good.' Crowninshield's gaze softened; grew faintly amused. 'I heard about the fight. They tell me you give a pretty good account of yourself with bare knuckles.'

'I tried to avoid it.'

But Crowninshield saw nothing good in this and said so. 'When a feller is in your fix, Mr Wheeler, he's got to prove himself. Avoidin' it doesn't settle anything. I'm glad I wasn't around. My job would've been to stop it—and I wouldn't have.' Crowninshield pocketed the warrants and patted the pocket.

'It's better that you get these people to respecting you a little before you ride with them,' he said, his facial expression shrewd and knowing. 'Otherwise—and it's happened plenty out here—you'd wind up with a slug in your back. Not from the Keystoners either.'

'They're pretty raunchy,' Bob said, meaning the settlers. 'Got their necks bowed and their hackles up, Sheriff.'

'Can you blame them?'

'I suppose not.'

'No. Neither could any honest man, Mr Wheeler. Those cattle are just about all they have—or had, I mean. There'll be some tucked-

76

up bellies by fall if they don't get them back—
or the money for them—one or the other.'

'What do you plan to do?'

'First, I'll ride to Kearney, show the warrants to Sheriff Martin over there. Then,
whether he'll come along or not I'll go out to
Keystone and serve 'em.'

'Alone?' asked Bob, raising his eyes to
Crowninshield's countenance.

'No,' the sheriff answered drawlingly. 'Not
alone. I'd like to have you along, only I'm
afraid, if any trouble started, they'd pick you
off first thing. Cullen an' Cartwright are smart;
they'll know right off who the witness is against
them.'

'They'll guess quick enough,' agreed Bob.

'So—I'll take some local boys.'

'I'll go.'

Crowninshield considered this a brief moment, then spoke again. 'You'll be spreadin'
yourself around kind of thin, Mr Wheeler.
You'll be takin' chances you don't have to
take.'

'I've got other reasons.'

'I see. Well; like I said, Mr Wheeler; I can't
take part in a private feud. I don't even want
to be around when it happens.'

Bob arose, shrugged and turned doorward.
'The chips will fall as they will,' he told the

lawman. 'I can't control that. When do you want to leave?'

'I think tonight. I think we'll stand a better chance at night. Not so easy to bushwhack folks in the dark.'

'I'll get a horse and meet you in front of the office.'

The sheriff nodded but made no immediate move to rise or leave the café. As Bob passed out into the smoky mistiness of lowering dusk, Crowninshield called the café proprietor to him.

'I want a posse,' he said to the nondescript man behind the counter. 'Pass the word around, Jake.' Sheriff Crowninshield arose finally. 'And you might as well tell the boys this won't be any picnic.' Then he, too, left the café.

New Hope, squatting as it did low upon the Nevada soil, was only slightly more ugly than Kearney, which, having been there longer, had at least a few trees; a little shade and comfort within its boundaries. But New Hope had something Bob saw as he slouched in the dusk now, waiting for the hostler to saddle a horse for him, that Kearney lacked. This was a more feasible access route to the more northerly towns where business and prosperity lay. He wondered idly if, before too many more years had passed, New Hope would not altogether eclipse the cow town of Kearney. He also considered it likely that after Keystone's grip was broken, more settlers would come. That was how it had happened in Nebraska Territory where farms flourished now athwart the old trails and holding grounds, and while he had been raised in the old traditions of the cattlemen he felt no ardent loyalty to the things which usually kept range men bound tightly together; he had never, in fact, been an owner, and for the last five years he had not even been a rider.

Lamplight began to glow and the furious heat drew off, leaving the soil to sigh with a faint-heeded breeze as full night descended. He took the fresh horse, when it was brought up, and led it thoughtfully down where Sheriff Crowninshield's sturdy silhouette was moving among gathering horsemen. After this night, he mused, it might be possible for a man to take up his interrupted life again. Until it ended it did no good to search ahead for signs. This was the flowing course of violence and of danger—and death. A man could do no more than remain alert and prepared; beyond that he must react to each separate second with all that was in him, if he was to survive at all.

They left New Hope as the tilted moon began

its ascent; twelve men on horses more accustomed to harness than to saddlery. But grimly resolute men; the kind of men who went down to their deaths stubbornly and unyieldingly; the most difficult kind of men to overcome.

Riding ahead with Charley Crowninshield, Bob said he did not think the settlers were adequately armed. To this the sheriff made reply only after a long look backwards at his following posse.

'If they had pistols instead of shotguns,' he said, 'not one in five would be accurate with 'em. There are some buffalo rifles amongst 'em too. Mr Wheeler; did you ever see a man after a buffalo slug hit him?' Crowninshield shook his head without awaiting an answer. 'Doggonedest mess you ever saw. No; I think for the kind of men they are, they couldn't be better armed.'

For a while there was only desultory talk behind Bob Wheeler and Sheriff Crowninshield. The settler posse-men were too full of their concern to be loquacious this night. Their horses made more noise than they did.

'There probably won't be any fight anyway,' Crowninshield said suddenly, putting his uppermost thoughts and speculations into words.

Bob glanced over at him. He did not think

the sheriff believed what he had just said, but it was too dark to make out whether or not the lawman's features showed a flaw in their expression to prove this. He said: 'Sheriff, Keystone has no less than eighteen riders. The cutting crew alone could eat these squatters of yours for breakfast any day in the week, given no more than an even chance.' He paused. 'There'll be a fight and I think you know it, too. Cullen, Cartwright, Butch Barlow and the others won't let you take them back to a settler town to be tried. That'll be the same as giving you permission to hang them and they know it.'

'I don't figure to take them back to New Hope,' replied Crowninshield. 'We'll lock them up in Kearney.'

'Aren't you afraid their boys will break them out?'

Crowninshield puckered his lips up and blew out a diminishing breath. 'No. We'll bed down there after the men are locked up. Anyway; Sheriff Martin wouldn't hold still for bustin' prisoners out of his jail.' Crowninshield yawned prodigiously, spat aside and cleared his throat.

'They'll be tried over there anyway. That's where the circuit judge'll hold court next time he's through the countryside. It's handier for him because he lives over there.'

Bob's rejoinder sounded cynical. 'It'd be handy all right,' he said, 'having the judge live in your town.'

Crowninshield shook his head at that. 'Not like you mean. Not this judge. When men have to be tried Judge McDonald is less likely to be influenced than anyone I ever ran across. He's about as fair a—'

'McDonald?'

Crowninshield paused long enough to throw a look at his riding mate. 'You know him?' he asked.

Bob rode for a time without answering. He removed his hat, scratched his head and replaced the hat. 'Does he live west of Kearney in a big white house with a horse-shed out back?'

'That's him.'

'I'll be damned!'

Crowninshield continued to gaze at Bob. 'What's the trouble?' he queried finally, attempting to define for himself the peculiar expression Wheeler's face reflected.

'No trouble. I just hid out in his horse-shed when Keystone was after me, is all.'

'Well; that's no crime.'

'And he's got a daughter named Aimee.'

'That's right. Prettiest gal in Nevada, to my notion.'

Bob cleared his throat, reached automatically for his tobacco sack and began twisting up a cigarette. When he had told her he thought Keystone owned the law she had bent a gravely searching look upon him. Remembering that now, he flushed in the darkness.

She had said they would meet again and there had been conviction in her voice too. His neck reddened in recollection. Of course. She had known that men in trouble in the Kearney country eventually crossed her father's path; that was why she had spoken with such conviction.

He exhaled smoke in a long, outward sweep of breath. And the kiss. He moved self-consciously in the saddle. In this respect, though, his memory was very vivid. He recalled now without effort that she had returned the pressure of his rough lips with equal fervour. It ameliorated his acute discomfort, remembering this now, but it did not allay his sense of embarrassment. He said again: 'I'll be damned.'

This time though, Sheriff Crowninshield merely shrugged. His thoughts were elsewhere.

CHAPTER SEVEN

They rode into Kearney from the west arriving there after full darkness was down. Very few words were spoken among them and the obviously uneasy squatters held close to Charley Crowninshield. He, in turn, made his horse fast to the rail behind him, then turned for a slow and thoughtful scrutiny of the town. Bob, watching him from the edge of his vision, thought he saw a flaw in the older man's complete self-assurance. Crowninshield was in no hurry to leave the hitchrail.

The sheriff's roving glance fell upon Bob; he caught the analytical gaze which was upon him and he hitched up his shell-belt.

'You want to come with me to Jack Martin's office?' he queried.

Without replying Bob pushed forward. Crowninshield moved after him tossing words over his shoulder to the posse-men. 'Stay with the horses,' he said crisply. 'We'll be right back.'

Nearing the office of Kearney's law, Bob slowed. 'If he doesn't recognise those warrants or won't get involved he'll likely send someone on ahead to warn Cullen and Cartwright, won't he?'

Crowninshield frowned over his answer. 'I don't know. I kind of doubt it. This is Keystone's town but I know for a fact that Jack Martin's arrested his share of Keystoners.'

'Yeah. For being drunk and disorderly, maybe. But this is different.'

Crowninshield stopped. He stood wide-legged, gazing ahead at the office door of Kearney's law where lamplight showed. His frown deepened and he did not speak right away. Then he made a thrusting shrug with his shoulder-points and moved out again.

'It's up to him,' he told Bob, his voice hardening. 'We've got our duty to do an' if he don't do his—that's something else altogether. Come on.'

This, thought Bob, was the way he had expected New Hope's rugged lawman to act. He moved out in support of Charley Crowninshield. They entered Sheriff Jack Martin's office side by side.

The man within the small office was eating from a tin plate at a battered roll-top desk. He looked quickly upwards, his field of vision taking in, first of all, the presence of his visitors, secondly their resolute expressions and finally, with widening interest the ivory-stocked gun and the general appearance of the younger of them. Sheriff Martin very carefully put his fork down, turned quietly in his chair and nodded.

'Hello, Charley,' he said in an inflexionless voice.

'Hello, Jack. This here is Bob Wheeler.'

Sheriff Martin nodded woodenly. Bob knew he had been recognised; that Sheriff Martin was carefully fitting him into some preconceived niche within his mind. 'Howdy,' he said, in the same flat, emotionless tone.

He swung back towards Crowninshield, his eyes holding steadily to the other lawman's face. 'What's on your mind, Charley?'

Crowninshield reached inside his coat, drew forth the warrants and put them gently upon Martin's desk. 'These,' he said, adding nothing to it.

Martin looked long at the warrants. His face paled a little in the lamplight. After several moments he turned, fixed a strong stare on Bob, then spoke as his attention was switched to Crowninshield.

'Do you know what you're doing, Charley?' he queried quietly. 'You got Keystone's top men here. Harold Cullen, Eb Cartwright, Butch Barlow, Reno Carson, Dusty, Turk and a passel of John Does. You also got Mike Barlow who's not a Keystone man at all.'

At Martin's last words Bob spoke up. 'Mike Barlow is wanted for murder at Blockton, Nebraska.'

Martin's expressionless eyes swung back. 'I hadn't heard anything about that,' he said.

'You would have,' retorted Bob, 'if you'd wired Tim Beasley about it at Blockton like you wired him about me.'

Martin sat perfectly still for a long time. Finally he faced back towards the warrants on his desk and renewed his study of them. Without looking up he said to Crowninshield: 'Charley; you aim to serve these things tonight?'

'As soon as we leave your office,' Crowninshield answered, his eyes unwaveringly on Martin's profile. 'The reason I brought 'em here is because this is your area, Jack. By rights it's up to you to serve them.'

'Yeah,' Martin said softly, drawling the word with a slowness Bob thought full of reluctance. He very gradually let his body turn loose in the chair and slump. He faced towards Crowninshield again and this time there was no mistaking the pain in his glance.

'You got a posse, Charley?'

'Yes.'

'Squatters?'

'Settlers, yes. What's the difference?'

Martin began to gently wag his head. 'Key-

87

stone won't let squatters ride up and arrest its top men, Charley. There'll be blood spilt.'

For a short space of time there was no more talk. The sound of Sheriff Martin's breathing was loud in the office.

Bob straightened up off the wall. Beside him, Charley Crowninshield also drew up, moved to action by Wheeler's movement.

'You coming along?' he quietly asked Jack Martin.

'I guess I got to, Charley.' Martin got up slowly, held out the warrants of arrest to Crowninshield, and reached for his hat. 'I reckon you know this is goin' to split my county wide open, don't you?'

Crowninshield nodded, his jaw locked closed.

'And if you can't make your charges stick, Charley, the cowmen'll take the torch to your squatters...'

'I'm figuring on making it stick.'

Martin's dulled eyes went to bear directly upon Bob. 'He your only witness?' he queried.

Another short nod from Crowninshield.

At this Sheriff Martin walked to a wall-rack, took down a carbine and shotgun, one in each hand, and started past toward the door without speaking again or looking at either of his visitors. His thoughts, though, were as obvious as though he had shouted them. He believed

Bob Wheeler was as good as dead.

'Jack?' Crowninshield called quietly as they were following Martin north along the plank-walk.

'Yeah?'

'You going to take some Kearney men with you?'

Martin shook his head. 'I dassen't' he answered. 'If I made up a posse here some-one'd ride hell-for-leather to Keystone before we were clear of town. If this can be done, Charley, I'd like to make it come off without shooting.'

Bob, until Martin spoke those words, had been unable to make up his mind about Kearney's lawman. Now he looked at Crownin-shield, caught the older man's silent nod, and nodded back. Keystone obviously did not own Sheriff Jack Martin, in spite of his obvious reluctance to do what he must now attempt to accomplish. This was a weight lifted from Bob's shoulders.

The New Hope posse-men eyed Sheriff Martin askance saying nothing. They got back astride in deep silence, waiting for Crownin-shield to jerk his head at them, then wheeled out behind Wheeler, Crowninshield and Martin.

The horse of Jack Martin, a leggy grulla

gelding, had been patiently awaiting his nightly unsaddling at the hitchrail where the New Hope men had tied up. He seemed now to resent being ridden out, and Martin, his carbine booted but the shotgun balanced across his lap, swore fiercely at him before the animal settled down into a begrudging walk northward.

To break the awkwardness Bob said, 'He's a mite barn-sour tonight, sheriff.'

Martin made a toneless reply; his thoughts were clearly not on the animal. 'He usually don't have to go out of town after dusk, Mr Wheeler. He's like a lot of men I know. Gets used to his private habits and don't like to be shook out of them.'

The thickening moon arose with silent majesty to push outward and downward its flaring silver light. Around the moving body of silent horsemen the desert lay softly lovely this night, with little to break its wide and endless sweep except for occasional clumps of stunted sage and buck-brush—the latter a name applied by range men to any of the infinitely varied and nondescript scraggles of undergrowth upon which deer were known to browse.

Out of the stillness, broken only by muffled hoofbeats, came the sudden-soft voice of Charley Crowninshield. 'I know how you feel,' he told Jack Martin, 'but this thing couldn't go on indefinitely, Jack. Keystone's been rustling settler-beef wholesale lately.'

'I don't see why they'd do that, Charley,' Martin said in mild protest. 'They got more beef than you can shake a stick at.'

Bob spoke out: 'I was told Keystone figured it could break squatters easier than it could fight them.'

Martin turned this over in his mind. 'I see,' he eventually murmured. 'By runnin' off their beef?'

'Yes.'

'It's a new wrinkle in squatter-cowmen relations,' Martin turned for the first time since they had left Kearney to look squarely at Bob Wheeler. 'You know for a fact they've done this?'

'For a fact Sheriff. I even helped them.'

Martin's unblinking gaze remained fixed and again Bob had no trouble divining his thoughts. He felt his face darkening in spite of himself.

'I owe Keystone no loyalty,' he said.

'You took their money, didn't you?'

'Not a dime. I worked for them a week and I hired out between pay periods.'

'But you worked for them. You ate their grub.'

Bob's retort was curt. 'Sheriff; it seems to

91

me you are having trouble with your loyalties. When Keystone breaks the law it doesn't matter how big or how powerful or even how rich it is.'

Jack Martin faced forward and said no more. Sheriff Crowninshield, who had purposely kept his eyes off either man during this exchange, now began to work up a cigarette. When it was going he said, to no one in particular. 'Can't be much farther now.'

It wasn't much farther and Bob's alertness increased as they crossed familiar cattle trails, passed alkali sinks and ancient depressions where buffalo had once wallowed to free themselves of lice and ticks. Behind him rode the posse-men, only now and then mumbling among themselves, sensing, it seemed, a nearing of the end of their trail, the rattle of their horses' hoofs against the increasing stoniness of the underfooting loud in the night.

Bob's thoughts went on ahead; he thought that by now the drive would be made up; that very possibly Barlow's cutting crew would be homing at the headquarters ranch. This would also mean that most of Keystone's other cowboys would be there also. He had never learned the total number of riders Keystone had on its payroll but he thought, considering the size of the herds, the thousands of acres to be

92

patrolled, and the amount of riding which had to be done on so immense a ranch, that there could be no less than eighteen and perhaps no more than twenty-five riders, full-time.

It was not a pleasant reflection, and while he hoped right along with Sheriff Martin that there would be no shooting, also like Martin, he was far from sure about this, and for the same reason. He could not imagine Harold Cullen or Butch Barlow surrendering meekly to a posse of hoe-men in cracked boots, floppy old hats, and mounted on horses showing collar marks instead of saddle scars.

Finally, as they were nearing the place on the plain where it would be possible to see Keystone's darkly low and strong-made buildings, Bob's mind drew off for the last time and closed down upon other things. The memory, for instance, of a smiling boy's laughter; of his confident gaze upon a life without complications; and finally, of his death at a card table in another trail-town hundreds of miles away, for a lack of tact which was endemic in youth. He had beaten a card-shark at poker and had laughed his triumph. The next moment he was stained-scarlet-dead from a .44 slug and his furious killer was gone, riding his horse like a man possessed and burning up the trails away from Nebraska to Nevada, fearful in the full knowledge that the boy he had killed had been unarmed.

Twenty-seven days of trailing, Bob reflected now, and nearly that many more days after locating his brother's murderer wading hip-deep in the troubles of others when all he'd come here to do was kill a murderer. A simple world had unexpectedly turned into one with a thousand sides and colours; into an environment he was now too deeply involved with to get clear, and there were now other compounding questions, seemingly endless, and each of them rang in his mind like footsteps slowpacing an iron corridor.'

'There it is,' Crowninshield said abruptly, halting his horse. 'No lights showing, Wheeler.'

It required a moment to force his mind back to the present but Bob did it with his sense of urgency deepening. 'It's not that late,' he murmured, eyes fixed on the darkened buildings of Keystone. 'What time is it, anyway?'

A hoarse voice from behind spoke forward saying: 'Ten o'clock by my watch.'

Crowninshield's moonlighted face was turned sideways. 'You worked there,' he said to Wheeler. 'You got any ideas about this?' He was uneasy and was frank enough now, not to hide it from the others.

Bob, considering Jack Martin recalled now that Kearney's lawman had never once been out of his sight. When this might have re-assured him it did not; he considered it likely now that word of the posse's coming might even have come from New Hope itself, where the people knew, and were fiercely pleased at what was in process of happening.

He freed himself of these speculations though; they were not pertinent at this juncture. What mattered was those dark and silent buildings on ahead.

He said, without believing it himself. 'Maybe they've started the drive.'

Jack Martin said one word in rebuttal: 'No.' Then he cleared his throat, spat aside, and fixed a baleful stare ahead. 'The drive-herd's down near town at the edge of Keystone. They haven't started out with it yet.'

'They got word some way,' a settler muttered from behind. 'They're likely lyin' up there waitin' for us to ride into their yard.'

Charley Crowninshield looked uncertain again. Bob gauged this moment. Around him uneasiness was stirring. If they sat there much longer their resolution would dwindle. It was one thing to savagely condemn Keystone and its gun-handy crew from as distant a place as New Hope. It was another thing altogether to ride deliberately into the unblinking eyes of its many guns.

He lifted his reins and kneed-out. 'Come on; we've got warrants to serve.'

Around him horses moved out until gradually the entire posse was in motion again.

CHAPTER EIGHT

Against the night's utter hush and silver softness stars hung endlessly in the universe's
yeasty froth. A little stray breeze ran along
hoof-high carrying to the advancing horsemen
familiar smells of livestock and cooking fires.
Bob said quietly: 'Sheriff; hold up. Stay here.
I'm going in alone.'

Neither Crowninshield nor Martin objected
to this, and around them the posse-men alter-
nated their glances between the close-by dark
buildings and Bob Wheeler. They too, were
willing to learn more before going on.

He went on until the details of Harold
Cullen's long adobe house were clear, and the
ranch buildings also stood forth entirely as he
remembered them, then he dismounted and led
his horse forward, both caution and interest
coming to their peak in him. He did not, for
some inexplicable reason, feel fear.

He stopped still in the centre of Keystone's
yard swinging his glance from west to east.
When he would have moved closer to the house
he caught distantly the clatter of a ridden horse

coming strongly on from the west. He went swiftly to the barn area and stood there beyond any danger of an immediate sighting. The rider slowed to a long lope, the sounds of his passage through the night without echo, then both sound and horsemen came quickly into the yard sweeping onward towards the barn with unmistakable familiarity.

Bob saw the rider draw up at the barn, bend in the middle, he heard his saddle squeak and, as the horse fidgeted, the rider's garrulous voice call upon him profanely to hold still.

Bob strode into view leading his horse. He was holding his reins in his left hand; the right hand hung easy, inches from the ivory-butted sixgun.

'Hello, Jeb.'

The dismounted rider spun up into a rigid, peering posture, his scarred hand making the preparatory downward sweep.

'Don't do it, Jeb.'

'Huh? Who is it?'

'Me. Bob Smith.'

Jeb Arbuckle's hand moved well clear of the gun. 'Bob Wheeler, you mean,' the old man said explosively, letting all his pent-up startlement out in that short sentence. 'Jack Moffitt told us all who you were, boy. 'Recollect me askin' if you knew Moffitt?'

'I recollect, Jeb.'

'He was down in Nebraska with Mike Barlow. He spotted you the first night you rode into Kearney.'

'I wondered,' Bob said conversationally, 'how Cullen and Barlow found out.'

'Well. Now you know.' Jeb fidgeted with his reins. He became increasingly agitated under Bob's long stare. 'I tried to warn you,' he finally blurted at Bob. 'I told you they'd eat you alive if you crossed 'em, boy.'

Jeb, Bob thought, was uncommonly alert to his presence for some reason, and it was not, he felt sure, because the old rider had met him where he had expected to meet no one.

'What's troubling you?' he mildly asked keeping his eyes on the older man. 'Where've you been, Jeb?'

'Been? Just out ridin'. Lookin' for strays, boy.'

Bob strolled closer. 'In the dark?' he asked, weighing Arbuckle's every change in expression, suspecting something but uncertain what it was. 'Once more, Jeb: where have you been?'

'Told you, dang it. Ridin'.'

'Where are the others?'

'How the hell would I know? I'm just the chore-hand around here, boy. You know that. Nobody tells me—'

'Jeb, I want to tell you something. Beyond Cullen's house there is a posse with two sheriffs in charge of it. You did me a favour an' now I'm going to do you one.'

'A posse?'

'Yes.'

'So soon? God A'mighty, I told 'em it was crazy.'

'You want me to do you that favour, Jeb?' asked Bob, seeing the gust of frantic concern cross the older man's face. 'You want to ride out of here before the roof falls in?'

'I had nothin' to do with it, boy. You know I'm just an old man.'

'Start at the beginning,' said Bob, and instantly the old cowboy's voice spilt words, running on in the stillness of Keystone's empty yard.

'They figured you'd got over to New Hope with what you knew. Butch said they had to put an end to you before you stirred up the country ag'in 'em. Couple of the fellers figured, after you escaped 'em at Kearney, that you was so scairt you just lit out and never quit running. But Eb sided with Butch ag'in Mr Cullen. Eb was so mad at Cullen I thought it likely he'd call him out. By the time everyone knew who you were there were a couple of the steady riders draw their time and sashayed out

100

of the country. Didn't want to tangle with no fast-gun, they said. Then Cullen an' Cartwright an' Butch Barlow decided amongst 'em the only thing left to do was put the fear o' God into the squatters.'

'Why the squatters, Jeb?'

'Well, dammit all boy, they couldn't find you to kill you, and they knew you'd have the law on 'em directly, so they told us the only thing left to do was fix it so's those cussed squatters'd be too scairt to testify that they'd lost any critters. You understand?'

'I think so.'

'Sure you do. As soon as this night's work was over Butch and Mr Cullen was to light out with the drive. Get rid of it so's there'd be no squatter-critters for anyone to recognise, and by then there'd be no one willin' to testify anyway.' Jeb paused to sniffle and run a hand under his nose. 'And anyway,' he concluded, 'you wouldn't have hurt 'em very much because they'd have beaten the squatters with a full house in spite o' you.' Jeb paused, squinting into the southerly night. 'I don't see no posse,' he said, his voice firming up. 'I don't believe there's one out there.'

Bob's fingers locked around the old rider's arm, collaring his attention. 'What do you mean about this night's work, Jeb?'

Arbuckle's shifting gaze rose to Bob's face and stayed there. 'You already know that,' he said. 'You told me you did, boy.'

The grip tightened powerfully. 'Jeb; what are they doing tonight?'

Arbuckle twisted. 'Leggo, my arm, damn it.'

'Jeb; if you don't speak out you're going to jail and whatever's happened you'll be in it with Cullen and Cartwright and the others.'

'No! Slack off, will you; that's right painful.'

'Talk!'

'They rode out about sundown to burn New Hope out. Please let go my arm, boy.'

Bob's hand fell slowly away. He continued to regard Jeb Arbuckle through a moment of unbelieving stillness. Then he stepped across his horse and spun away without so much as a backward glance where Jeb stood massaging his arm and cursing.

Crowninshield and the others heard the insistent strong beat of his coming and were waiting, guns bared, when he cut in among them.

'Keystone's riding to burn New Hope out,' he cried, and gave them no second chance to hear but spurred on through them bearing swiftly into the west.

It required no more than a moment for Bob's message to penetrate. Then, before its frightening implications were wholly digested, the posse-men were racing after him bearing with them Sheriff Jack Martin of Kearney, whose blanched face looked death-like in this night's soft moon-glow.

Several hours later, with the first wild rush of their mounts cooling their faces, the posse-men slackened off; settled into a mile-eating, alternating running-walk and hard trot, and in this fashion covered the distance they had before them in good time. They made only one halt. That was when a man cried out: 'Ahead there, on the horizon.'

He said no more. He did not have to.

Against the velvet night a bloody glow showed low upon the horizon. Keystone had had too much of a head start. When several of the squatters would have whipped their horses into a killing run Bob's voice struck hard against them.

'Hold up! You'll only kill your horses and wind up on foot. *Hold up!*'

Not until Charley Crowninshield swung his mount to firmly bar the way of the foremost posse-man did the others draw rein. Crowninshield, his face livid and twisted, glared them down.

'You stay back where you belong,' he ordered, and fiercely cursed.

They continued forward with that writhing red light to guide them onward. When the last doubt vanished Kearney's lawman said weakly, 'Why? Whatever possessed them to do such a thing as that?'

No one made an answer.

They came into the first fragrance of burning wood at midnight. An hour later they came up out of the night bearing steadily into a thickening cloud of oily smoke. Then, close enough to recognise what remained, limned as it was by swirling flames, they could distinctly see bucket brigades battling the flames.

'I think,' said Sheriff Crowninshield heavily, 'that maybe Mr Martin better not ride in with us.'

'To hell with that,' a man ground out in a choking, despairing and hating tone. 'He's goin' to see what his Kearney cowmen done if I got to drag him along by the hair!'

Crowninshield said no more.

They came into New Hope from the south with a hot, roiled wind scorching their faces. Men appeared in the roadway shouting to them, pointing where the flames were fiercest and calling out. They rode past without heeding and did not draw up until they were near the red fury.

'You boys,' Sheriff Crowninshield told his

posse-men in a booming tone, 'join the bucket brigades. It looks like just the church and some of the other wooden buildings are going.' He put out a hand to brush fingers lightly over Bob's arm. 'Bring Martin to my office. I got to find someone and see if there were any witnesses.'

A flaming wooden wall creaked loudly and ominously. Men cried out in alarm and in warning. They scattered barely in time. The wall collapsed with a sound of tearing cloth and immediately afterwards an enormous spark-cloud rose straight up.

Bob leaned from the saddle to speak loudly against the flames' roaring and the loud cries of people standing near. To Sheriff Martin he said, 'Come with me,' and eased his mount around leading the way to Crowninshield's office, one of New Hope's many adobe buildings.

With the door closed behind them there came the less tumultuous noise of the furore outside. Jack Martin went to a chair and folded over into it. Colour returned only slowly to his cheeks and lips.

'There's got to be proof,' he said, tonelessly. 'It's no good simply saying Keystone did this.' When Bob, in the act of removing his hat and dropping wearily down upon a wall-bench, said nothing, Martin pushed out more words.

'Who told you they'd come over here?'

'Jeb Arbuckle, Keystone's chore-hand at the home ranch.'

'Oh.'

Martin sank deeper into gloom; he looked unseeingly at his hands and did not move again until Sheriff Crowninshield came through the door with four grimed and breathless men trailing in his wake. He shot Martin a bitter stare and spoke.

'Here are four men who traded shots with the Keystone. They got the best proof in the world it was Cullen's bunch.'

Martin looked up at the silent, waiting squatters. 'They saw 'em?' he said, making it half question, half statement.

Crowninshield turned and jerked his head. 'Fetch him in,' he said through lips that scarcely moved.

Another squatter came into the room. At arm's distance before him, being pushed savagely, was a man Bob recognised instantly; Reno Carson; who had dreamed of going down to San Francisco to buck the faro games. Carson had a bandaged head and a badly swollen jaw. He groped his way to a vacant chair and fell into it. He did not see Bob Wheeler until, moments later, when the condemning silence became unendurable, he raised his eyes.

106

'Hello, Reno,' said Bob, his face, alone of all those in that room showing no murder in its eyes with the exception of Kearney's lawman.

'Who led you over here?'

'Cullen an' Cartwright an' Butch.'

'Did they promise you another bonus?'

Carson shook his head like it was a bowl full to the brim; as though he dared not spill a drop of its contents. 'They said we had to do it, is all. Otherwise, when the law came, the squatters'd be brave enough to talk against us.'

'What happened to you?'

'Some squatter shot my horse from under me with a buffalo gun. When I was gettin' up they liked to killed me—a dozen or so of 'em. Someone tried to shoot me. I turned my head just in time.'

'You'll live to wish they had killed you,' a settler spat at Reno Carson.

Crowninshield turned a cold stare upon the speaker, silencing him in this fashion. He then leaned a little from the waist to touch Jack Martin's shoulder briefly. 'You satisfied?' he asked. 'You think they'll wiggle out of this, Jack?'

Sheriff Martin drew himself upright with a visible effort, and for the first time in hours his voice sounded firmly resolute, as though he had at long last made up his mind about something.

'No; but I think the longer we sit around here the less chance we stand of gettin' them all, Charley, and gettin' just Cullen an' maybe Barlow or Cartwright isn't going to be enough. The governor an' the army'll hear about this by morning. We got to move out.' He stood up, let off a long breath and looked steadily at Crowninshield. 'We've got to have fresh horses.'

Bob also stood up. When Crowninshield looked his way Bob nodded.

'All right,' Crowninshield said, turning to face the silent settlers. 'The keys are in my desk; lock this Keystoner up in one of the cells and go round me up some fresh men and three fresh horses.'

Bob interrupted here, thinking ahead. 'Never mind the men,' he exclaimed. 'Just get the fresh mounts.' When the settlers looked away from him towards Crowninshield, obviously unwilling to obey Wheeler, Bob spoke his fears. 'It will be just as bad as burning a town if, when we catch them, Sheriff, the posse-men lynch them.'

'There's too much country to cover by ourselves,' protested Crowninshield, making an impatient gesture with one arm.

'We'll take Kearney men this time,' said Bob. 'Let their own kind run them to earth.

It'll help prove to these people all cowmen aren't night-riders, too.'

'He's right,' spoke up Sheriff Martin. 'He's plumb right.'

CHAPTER NINE

Freshly mounted, Bob rode with Crownin-shield and Jack Martin back to Kearney. They arrived there shortly before first light and when the lawmen left to round up their posse, Bob was accosted from the gloom by a voice he instantly recognised, and which belonged to a man whom he had thought would be long gone by that time, and still riding. Jeb Arbuckle.

'Come out where I can see you,' he said, in response to the old rider's quick call from the shadows.

'Kearney's got too many eyes for that, even at this hour,' answered old Jeb. 'Listen to me, boy; the men you want came back to the ranch a couple of hours after you left. They took fresh mounts and lit out.'

'Where to?'

'Cartwright and the Barlow brothers for over the line into California.'

'With the drive?' Bob asked, incredulously, thinking of that jagged, seemingly endless mountain drive down into California over the Sierras.

'No, dammit all,' snapped Jeb impatiently, still not stepping out where he could be seen. 'They're leavin' the drive.'

'Jeb; back at the Keystone you said—'

'I know what I said, boy. But that was before they found out a posse was after 'em.'

Bob was instantly struck by two dissimilar thoughts. He made a question of the foremost one. 'How did they find that out?'

Arbuckle's answer was a while coming. Finally he said, 'I told 'em. I had to, boy. I was soakin' my arm in salts when they come back to the ranch. They asked me who was there—who put them finger marks on my arm. I had to tell 'em.'

'Sure,' said Bob sardonically. 'You had to tell them about the posse too.' He flung up his reins, toed into the stirrup and rose up to settle into his saddle. 'Why are you telling me this now, Jeb?'

'So's you'll know which side o' the law I'm on.'

'All right, Jeb. I'll remember. One more question: which trail were they taking?'

'Butch and Eb weren't sure. That's why they come here first and rousted up Butch's brother. He's been over most every trail through the cussed mountains. He said they'd best go the old *arriero* trail, north of the old

Hastings Cutoff.'

Bob swung his head to see the length and breadth of Kearney's main thoroughfare. It was empty of movement everywhere he looked. 'Jeb?' he called, a moment later.

'Yeah?'

'When those fellers I rode in with come back, tell them I've gone after the Barlows and Cartwright. Tell them to concentrate on Harold Cullen and the others; that I'll be back when I'm through doing what I've got to do.'

'Sure,' the old rider said from his position in the dark passageway between two buildings, and later, after Bob was riding southward in a swinging gait, he cackled to himself saying gleefully aloud: *'If* you come back, boy, not when. 'Cause I'll lay odds of fifty-to-one you ain't never coming back.'

With no knowledge at all where he would strike the fugitives' trail but unwilling to wait for daylight in order to ascertain where it lay, Bob rode steadily southward. He knew that the Barlows and Eb Cartwright would also be riding in that general direction for the elemental reason that California was south of Nevada. It was not much to use as a guide and he was unsure, also, whether there would be towns along his way where he might pick up news of the passing of three hurrying strangers. But a man who had been so long on a quest invariably felt as Bob Wheeler now did; any action, even wrong action, was better than no action at all.

The sun was climbing overhead before he struck some rolling swales, indicative of more prominent upthrusts ahead. It was fully overhead hanging in a faded, brassy sky when he topped out over a gravelly ridge and came upon a set of weathered buildings. There, an ancient widower anxious for company told him where the *arriero* trail was, then enlarged upon his information by reciting long-windedly how he distinctly recalled, as a youth, seeing the dark and brilliant-eyed Spanish *arrieros*—packers—come down out of the far-away mountains driving, sometimes leading, their long strings of pack animals, loaded down with the treasure of the mines or the baubles of the seacoast.

Bob pushed ahead hurryingly after that, seeking to cut the *arriero* trail ahead of nightfall because the old man had told him he was a long way east of it.

There were several other ranches; he considered canvassing them for news of strangers passing, but did not. Unless the Barlows and Eb Cartwright branched off farther along he would find them sooner or later, and there was, therefore, no point in stopping to ask more questions; no point in losing more time.

He bedded that night beneath the first full blown tree he had encountered since leaving Kearney; it was a red fir growing boldly—and inexplicably—far north of the Sierras. A great, ragged precursor of what lay ahead in the nearing purple mountains.

The next day, with mountain-shoulders sloping downward towards him on both sides cramping the dim old trail, he cut sign of fresh-made tracks and before noon struck a fluted pass where cool wind funnelled endlessly, bearing to him the fragrance of expiring coals and black-oak ashes. He found the camp and wasted precious moments quartering it; drawing up from the trampled soil three boot-marks, three faint impressions where bed-rolls had held tired men the night before, and the southerly continuing sign of three shod horses moving ahead.

His second night out, coming in a slow lope around a long-spending curve where a wealth of lasting shadows lay, he emerged into sight of a decrepit little town, clearly left over from the long-gone years of the Gold Rush. He had, in his lifetime, run across other ghost towns, but usually they had no smoke rising from a chimney like this one did. He loosened his holstered gun and let a hand lie lightly upon it, then prodded his animal forward tracing out even in the gathering night that the old trail went straightaway through the village and continued its plunging run southward.

Most of the little town's buildings were no longer safe to enter. Many were tumbled down and in process of collapsing but on either side of the trail, which was here widened into a respectability which might be called a road, there were several buildings which showed unmistakably the recent labours of human, not ghostly, hands. Additionally, when Bob's mount's shod hoofs struck down ringingly upon a granite crust, from somewhere beyond his sight in the village came a horse's eager whinny.

A ghost town this might be, he told his horse in a whisper, but there were more than ghosts in it this night.

He approached the town anglingly and did not see lamplight until he ascertained which old building had the firelight coming from its chimney. He rode directly to it, mindful that three sets of eyes might be watching for pursuit, swung off and looped his reins. There was not a sound to be heard now, but neither was that feeling in the night a wary man could sense. He left the horse, approached the lighted building, and first peered through a grimy window. There was a man eating from a bowl behind an ancient bar. There were two more men seated at a table playing cards. All three were grizzled. From their attire they appeared to be hard-rock miners. None, he saw, were the men he sought.

When he pushed in out of the night three heads came alertly up; three sets of eyes clung to him with dead steadiness. The man at the bar moved first; he pushed away his bowl, wiped both hands flatly on his shirtfront and nodded without geniality or welcome.

'Drink?' he asked, studying Bob as the latter crossed the room.

'And something to eat,' said the Nebraskan quietly, taking up the glass when it was filled, turning his back deliberately and sending a level gaze at the card players. They looked away, returning to their game, but in a way that fairly screamed their otherwise thoughts.

'I got slow-elk or canned beef,' the barman said.

Bob, with little taste for venison said, 'Canned beef.' He turned back to face the barman, 'and some information.'

'Yes,' the miner said, in a tone so false Bob did not ask his question, but held the man's eyes with his own for a long enough period for the miner to understand he would know a lie if it was told him.

'You had some men through here today.'

He could hear the card players shifting in their chairs; knew their stares were again upon him from behind.

'How long ago were they here?'

'I was up on my claim all day,' the barman said without letting his eyes stray. 'Maybe someone was through here although it ain't too likely. Not many folks come through the mountains here any more.'

'The tracks led here, mister.'

'I can't help that. Like I said, I was up on my claim all day. 'Town ain't visible from up there.'

Bob turned towards the card players. 'You fellers were up on your claims too?' he asked, the irony strong in each word.

'Yup,' one of the men at the table said.

The other one simply nodded. Both became very intent upon their game.

Bob drew away from the bar. 'Fix the beef,' he ordered. 'I'll put up my horse and be back.'

But he did not immediately afterwards return to the saloon. He went instead in search of the horse that had nickered, found him favouring an injured leg and examined him closely in the darkness. The animal was superficially skinned all along his right side, as though he had fallen in the rocks. It took only a moment for Bob's experienced hand to trace out the Keystone brand on his left shoulder.

He made an additional search of the town's corrals, barns and sheds but found no other horses. He then returned to the bar-room, found his supper ready, took it to a wall table and ate leisurely with his back against solid wood.

One of them was here. Evidently, when the horse had fallen, one of them had been injured and his companions had left him behind in their hurrying travels.

When the meal was finished Bob curled up a cigarette and thoughtfully smoked it. How much had the injured man paid these miners to keep their silence? Which one, in his absence, had gone stealthily to warn the injured man in his hiding place that a stranger had just ridden in seeking three horsemen?

He had no money to offer the three miners, nor had he a single doubt but that somewhere in the night a cocked gun was awaiting his appearance in the moonlight. He finished the cigarette, took his plate and cup back to the bar and set them in front of the barman. Assessing the man's face, which was not strong nor principled, it occurred to him that his only foe was not watching him from some tumble-down shack out in the night. In these mountains there was no law; men had been secretly killed for less than Bob Wheeler possessed—a saddle, a horse, a gun, and perhaps a few dollars.

'I knew a man once,' he told the barkeep, his gaze steady, his voice convincing, 'who loved money so much he'd take any man's side so long as he got a few dollars.'

The barman's coarse features were briefly impassive, then they began to darken into a scowl. 'You did, huh?' he said, facing Bob's quiet warning without fear.

'Yeah. 'You know what came of him? He got between a murderer and the man who was after him one time—and his wife turned up a widow.'

The barman's gaze clouded. He looked beyond Bob to the card table and back again.

'You see that stuffed owl over the door?' asked Bob turning slightly to face doorward. 'That glass eye of his—the left one—it looks treacherous, doesn't it?'

There came no visible movement, just the deafening roar of the ivory-butted gun, made doubly loud by four walls. The stuffed owl's left eye disappeared in a puff of dust. The bird quivered on its false perch.

'That,' Bob said mildly, 'could have been an accident.' He waited but the barman, and the card players as well, had nothing at all to

119

say. 'He doesn't look right with just one eye.'
Again, with a blur that defied watching the sixgun tilted inches from its holster, lashed out-
wards and upwards with a tongue of orange
flame, and again the moth-eaten old stuffed owl
shook from impact. He was now eyeless.

One of the card players put his pasteboards
down gently upon the table, pushed back his
chair and rose. Without looking at anyone he
started away. 'I got to feed my mules,' he said,
and strode swiftly out of the saloon.

Bob gazed at the remaining miner. He also
arose. 'See you tomorrow, maybe,' he told the
barman, and walked purposefully doorward.

When they were alone the saloonman put
both hands upon the bar-top and kept them
there in plain sight. He said to Bob: 'You win,
mister. Do you want to know where he is?'

'No. He paid you not to tell me, didn't he?'

'Yes.'

'A man sleeps better if he doesn't have to
remember betraying someone's trust.'

'That's a fact, mister.' The barman's face
softened with relief. 'Is he a murderer?'

'That and more. He and his friends burnt
New Hope couple days ago.'

This impressed the miner. 'Burnt it?' he
said, his voice rising.

'He killed an eighteen-year-old unarmed kid.
120

I want him for that—not for burning a squatter-town.'

The barman leaned upon the bar eyeing his hands reflectively. 'He give us twenty dollars, mister. His two friends ain't no more'n four hours ahead of you. They'll bed down along the trail. One of 'em knows the mountains but the other one, the skinny feller, don't.'

From this Bob knew which fugitive was in the ghost town. 'Twenty dollars is a strong incentive,' he said to the fat miner. 'Twenty dollars might incline a man to hide in the darkness with his carbine. It might inspire his miner-friends to do likewise.'

The barman glanced at the eyeless owl. 'No,' he retorted with full frankness, 'it ain't enough money to get killed over. No, mister; and them other two fellers got claims up the mountainside a mile or so. They won't come down here again until all the shooting's over.'

'And you?'

'I got a claim up there too. I was just fixin' to leave when you rode in.'

'I don't have any money to send along with you,' said Bob.

But the barman, casting another glance towards the stuffed owl, said with reassuring swiftness: 'That ain't necessary. Not necessary at all, mister.' He started around the bar. 'You

know; once when I was a youngster over at
Dodge City, I seen a man shoot like that.' He
turned from the doorway and nodded. 'Good
night, mister. Good hunting.'

CHAPTER TEN

The little town lay deathly hushed in the moonlight. Bob went easily out through the saloon's door and considered. The fugitive who knew these mountains—which would be Mike Barlow—and the skinny fellow—which would be Eb Cartwright—had left Butch to what they undoubtedly thought was a destiny of no immediate peril.

But Butch by now knew differently and no matter how painful his injuries he would wish to rejoin his friends.

Bob cut to his right along the rotten plankwalk. He held to shadows and stopped frequently to listen. From the moon-washed reflection of an east-west roadway he heard distinctly the soft crush of booted feet moving around behind the buildings which cut off his view. He glided briefly into moonlight then came again into gloom as he moved swiftly in the direction of that brief hurrying sound of a man's passage.

Behind the saloon and its adjoining buildings was the place where he had located the corralled

Keystone horse. But here, with squared shadows lying layered upon one another from the standing mountains to the rear and the equally obscuring buildings in front, no moonlight penetrated.

He stood stone-like in that drowning blackness straining for a shifting silhouette. When it came it was the Keystone horse; he was moving within his corral with an uneasiness any born horseman would have instantly understood; he was not alone out there.

A murky shape firmed up in the gloom. It was moving with difficulty toward the horse. There was a very faint lustre to an extra bulkiness around it. There came also the faint drag of a cinch-ring in the dust, the scuff of flopping stirrups.

Bob called softly forward: 'Butch!'

There came then the solid sound of something heavy striking the ground, a moment of total silence then, farther back, another familiar sound; the kind made by rickety corral stringers being pressured by a man's body squeezing through them.

'It won't do any good to run, Butch.'

Total silence closed down. The night ran on, the little town was strongly still and hushed in its faint-glowing moonlighted canyon.

Bob went forward, found the saddle, bridle

and blanket Butch Barlow had dropped, eyed the injured horse which in turn regarded him gravely from a wary distance, then Bob knelt in the dust and made two slashing motions with his pocketknife, severing both the front and rear cinchas.

He afterwards caught the horse, led him to the pole gate and released him on the gate's far side.

If Butch Barlow reached his friends this night it would not be by the same means he had employed to enter this nameless and lost mountain village, which meant he would not reach them at all because he and Bob Wheeler were alone here, Butch was injured, and his sole means of escape was now gone from him.

Bob returned to the saloon, carefully placed its solitary lantern where he could not be highlighted by it, and smoked a cigarette. He was in no hurry; he still had four or five hours to do what he must, before striking the southerly trail again. His horse was resting and he, himself, had no need for repose. He let an hour go by, then another hour. Then he left the saloon by a rear doorway and began a systematic search of the dark and empty buildings.

Butch Barlow was not on the east side of the roadway. Where moonlight shone upon dust, there were no fresh tracks. Neither was he beyond town, rearward. Bob made a wary patrol of the canyon back there. He had thought Butch might try for his own horse and saddle, but he had not. To make certain he could use neither, Bob hid his saddle and his bridle.

There remained only the west side of the road. There, Bob found the buildings were in even worse shape. There too, after midnight with the moon slanting away, its light pattern struck fully upon bleached wood and was reflected helpfully downward. Because of this Bob found the tracks he sought and he read them correctly.

Butch Barlow had an injured leg. He had fashioned a splint of sorts to it and each squiggle-mark in the dust showed where this rounded piece of wood struck ahead of a boot-print.

Because it was not possible to know which of the crumbling old shacks Barlow was hiding in, Bob went back a distance where a tumble of enormous boulders stood, and deliberately eliminated the least likely hiding places for the length of the block, with a careful study of them.

Behind him the moon was dropping swiftly now, making it appear that the full weight of the mountains tilted westerly. There was so great a depth of stillness his own breathing sounded harshly loud in the night. This waiting would further fray nerves set on edge by physical pain; Butch Barlow would be less of a man now than he had been at Keystone.

Taking up a handful of sharp-edged pieces of granite Bob went purposefully forward again, this time setting his wary course for a large, listing old building which might once have been an hotel or rooming house. At the last minute, informed by layers of smooth pale dust that Barlow was not in this old wreck, he crossed into the shadows of a rotting barn and went onward steadily passing in and out of lighted and dark intervals until, near the extreme southerly end of town, he found again the tell-tale squiggle marks.

Ahead of him was a foundationless miner's shack which had settled deeper into the soil until a grown man would have to bend low to enter.

There was a glassless window and a hanging rear door here, and out back what might once have been a chicken-house or a cow-shed. He made certain the shed was empty before putting it behind him, chucking a stone at the rear stoop, waiting as long as it took to move well clear of the shed, then chucking a second stone, this one gauged to strike a footstep closer to that yawning dark and doorless opening.

The night was blown apart by a lash of gunfire and the simultaneous explosion which accompanied it. On Bob's far left the cow-shed echoed from a tearing impact. Moonlight glowed whitely where Barlow's slug peeled off a long wooden splinter.

Bob unshipped his hand-gun cocked it and went forward deeper into the night. He chucked another stone aiming for this one to strike glancingly south of the door and near the ground. His aim was not good enough this time; the stone fell inches away from the siding. He dropped his remaining stones and flattened against the rough boards for a time, then began a cat-footed stalk forward towards the rear opening.

'Barlow,' he called, drawing down into a crouch. 'Listen, Barlow; I don't want to kill you. My fight's not with you. Come on out of there and leave your gun behind.'

Barlow's ragged voice came back in a vicious curse, then it paused to draw in breath and went on with less venom. 'You're after me all right, Wheeler, you damned liar. You want me bad enough.'

'For rustling and for burning New Hope, yes, but not as bad as I want your brother. Not badly enough to kill you.'

'What's the difference? I know what they'll do to me back at Kearney. Well, damn your meddlin' soul, Wheeler, you'll have to do it right here in this rotten hole. You won't take me back for no trial by a herd of squatters.'

'How bad are you hurt, Barlow?'

The dark man's voice turned cunning. 'Why don't you come in here and find out?'

Bob drew upwards slowly, holstered his gun and moved away. The night ran on as he moved along the shack's rear, cut easterly along one side wall and emerged around front where lengthening shadows were falling now farther out into the roadway. There, he laid his full weight upon both feet and began an inching progress toward that glassless front window. At the very most, he reasoned, the shack had no more than two rooms inside; the chance that the front window faced into the one concealing Barlow was as equally good as that it did not. But in his forward impetus and his narrowing concentration he stepped against a lying board and its complaining creak brought from within an instant shot.

'You got two left feet,' Barlow called tauntingly. 'They said you were a real terror with a gun, Wheeler. I'm beginnin' to doubt that.'

Bob stooped, caught up the board and tossed it through the window. Its diminishing clatter

129

echoed lingeringly but no shot came from within.

'That won't work either,' Barlow said, his tone changing away from the apprehension it had once held; turning now stronger with growing confidence. 'Try something else.'

Bob holstered his weapon, sought for some dead weeds in the moonlight, found them and carefully made a switch. 'All right,' he exclaimed. 'Maybe this'll do the trick.' He lit the weeds, held them lowered until the flames were licking upwards, then tossed the burning switch inside. 'That's a sample,' he called to Barlow. 'Just the same you'd better put it out. This shack'll go up like a haystack.'

There was a momentary bright flicker from beyond the window, then abrupt darkness.

'Come out now, Barlow. If I fire this place you may not get the chance.'

Butch Barlow's answer was in the same strong tone. 'All right, Wheeler. Do I get an even break?'

'You have my word on that.'

'Move out into the middle of the roadway then. Give me a chance to get clear first.'

Bob moved, but not roadward. He went back along the shack-front as far as the north edge of the building. There he waited, hearing from within the sounds of painful and slow movement. When Butch Barlow appeared finally, his pistol held at his side in one hand, his black glare raking the length of the roadway and finding no one there, he twisted slightly from the waist. He at once saw the weaving pattern of a moving man. It was Bob Wheeler cutting clear of the shadows, standing away from the shack in plain sight. Barlow's hand did not attempt to raise; it twisted at the wrist minimising movement yet bringing to bear the arcing gunbarrel. The Keystoner's hating gaze was bright with full confidence; his gun was free and moving, Wheeler's gun was holstered.

Then the blue-crimson burning lash of gunfire came from north along the roadway and Barlow's tipped barrel plunged drunkenly earthward and exploded thunderously kicking up a great gout of dirt and dust.

The stink of burnt powder became strong in the ensuing silence. Beyond the little town ran atrophying echoes. Butch Barlow leaned heavily against the door jamb trying with all his departing strength to lift his gun, to cock it for a second try. He could do neither. He looked, finally, into the pale, still face of his killer and that look of disbelief came over his features, exactly as Bob Wheeler had known it would come; exactly as he had seen it come to other glazing eyes.

Then Butch Barlow dropped his weapon, jack-knifed slowly in the middle and curled forward to drop solidly into the dirt, to lie there without moving.

Bob lingered long enough to take Barlow's wallet then walked in no hurry to his horse, saddled up and for the length of time required to re-load his pistol stood solemnly in the silent night. It had been, by all frontier standards, a fair fight; both men had fired; both had faced one another and in fact Barlow had had, as the oldtimers called it, 'the bulge'—the advantage. But in his heart Bob knew better.

He rode south beyond the ghost town without hurrying, thinking how the varieties of violent death had, in their final enactments, that one clear second when each man knew—but only one lived to recall—that there was no such thing as a fair gunfight.

The steely first palings before dawn found him a long way south and covering ground with a consuming gait. Where the pinched-down mountains drew back, once, he splattered through a mountain torrent and made good progress through a glade's tall grasses.

Two hours farther on he scented a cooking fire and traced out its strengthening fragrance only to discover it orginated from a log house set well back beyond sight of casual wayfarers.

He did not stop here; it was clear to him, the way that house was put beyond sighting, that its builder had no wish—perhaps with good reason—to be visited. He kept to the trail instead, watching for tracks and speculating idly on the number of wanted men living in seclusion in these mountains; thinking back to a time when he had run to earth his share of such men, and knowing from this past experience that these silent and lonely, and often saddened men, were no threat to anyone unless forced to become so.

The *arriero* trail began a gradual ascent into the red fir highlands. By high noon its snake-mottled meanderings twisted and turned into shade and sunlight. Far beyond, farther than a man could see, there lay a soft haze over endless saw-toothed ridges, some purple with distance, some red-gold and rusty with stair-steps of close-standing huge trees.

There were a thousand places for men to lose themselves in the Sierras, and as he rode along now Bob thought he would have attempted this if his place had been reversed with Mike Barlow. But from the tracks neither Barlow nor Eb Cartwright were thinking of anything but pushing onward as swiftly as they prudently could. Such, he told himself, was the confidence men possessed whose reliance upon themselves was above all other considerations. Neither Mike Barlow nor Eb Cartwright really feared pursuit; they simply wanted to avoid apprehension until a time when, possibly in some lawyer's office in San Francisco, they would agree to surrender to the law for a return to Kearney and trial. They would do this with a sneer and with the full weight of the book-law of city men supporting them.

At least for one of the men he was pursuing, though, Bob Wheeler had no intention of permitting this to happen. He had come too far, had ridden too many fresh and perilous trails to be denied the inflexible gun-justice which had formed and sustained him thus far in his lifetime.

When dusk came, moving up out of the canyons and arroyos instead of downward from the heat-faded heavens, he kept on. Even after nightfall and before the moon arose, at last fully rounded and enormous in its gliding ascent, he kept to his way, motivated by the certain knowledge that he was now very close to the men he sought.

Twice in this limitless world of vast distances and unknown side-trails he smelt smoke and neither time did he leave the trail to seek out the camps from which this came. He had another plan, and until the moon was dropping away, horizon-ward, on the far side of midnight, he made no stop at all.

Then he found a grassy clearing at the side of the trail, off-saddled, hobbled his horse, gathered up more dead-fall faggots than he would have needed if he'd had any food to cook, and built a fire of his own. He smoked a cigarette in its crackling brilliance, from time to time pushed more wood upon it so that reflected dancing red light twisted and writhed against the sombre darkness of surrounding big trees, then he put out his cigarette, took his blankets back beyond the first tier of forest and spread them upon a matting of ancient pine needles and sat down to wait.

CHAPTER ELEVEN

Sometimes a man who lived next to the earth and the earth's unchanging ways could, in the eleventh hour of his troubles, understand how these things would end. This had happened to Bob Wheeler but now, watching the moon-lighted trail beyond his clearing, and watching also the licking flames, he was uncommonly bothered by a feeling that all this was not going to come right for him.

He went forward once to build up his fire again, and he smoked another hand-made cigarette. He even, from his place back in the forest, examined his sixgun and returned it to his holster before sending aloft a searching glance for a clue to the time of morning.

There was a faint though persisting paleness off in the east. It did not widen swiftly but it gradually brightened through a spectrum of delicate colours until, around him, the mountains took on a metallic hue, then a salmon shade; a flowing, soft-filling of eternity with new daylight, until this uplands world in all its thin-aired hush came again as it always had, to the business of living a day at a time.

Woodchits walked incongruously wrong side up over tree trunks, pecking, probing and occasionally finding, the grubs they sought beneath rough pine bark. A fox appeared at the edge of the clearing. It stopped to test the air and consider his dying campfire with curiosity, and also with apprehension. It faded out noiselessly and Bob heard two horses coming along upon the trail beyond. He drew up off his blankets, stepped silently to the lee of a tree and waited. The riders halted; while one held an impatient beast upon rein the other rider veered off to pass over pine needles to the right of the trail. Bob moved off to intercept this man because he knew the stranger would see his horse before reaching the clearing. This was, he now thought, remembering his vague presentiment of the night before, what had been wrong; he had not anticipated Barlow and Cartwright being wary this far along. He had made a mistake in putting the horse where a scouting horseman might find him.

He listened to the very faint sounds of the oncoming rider, and hoped mightily it might be Mike Barlow. He had no feud with Cartwright; let the law run him to earth. If he could settle with Mike Barlow in this forest he would be content.

But his dilemma was simply that he could not watch both oncoming riders at the same time, hence one could pass his camp upon the yonder trail while he faced the other one, both of them alert to a human presence by the deliberately cultivated campfire he had laid to bring them to him.

From the forest's endless quiet he traced out his foeman's progress onward. Moving silently now to meet this man, he sighted both horse and rider at a distance and when he stopped, straining to identify the man, he failed because the horseman swung off on the far side, drew forth a carbine and passed beyond sight carefully moving so as to keep trees between himself and the camp his nose warned, was now quite close ahead.

Shifting position was no longer an easy matter; the stalking gunman was watching equally with Bob for any movement. But when the time arrived that he was safely cut off from a sighting Bob went with bold speed on an angle which eventually put him slightly behind the unidentified man. All he had to do next, was wait while his adversary continued stalking downward upon the clearing; this put Bob well behind him.

Then the stranger saw Bob's horse cropping bunch-grass and froze. Behind him, Wheeler had only a shadowed profile to study; it was not yet enough.

Very quietly the man, carbine up now in both hands, ready but as yet un-cocked, glided closer to the horse. When he finally stopped altogether it was glaringly clear he knew whose horse he was staring at.

Bob could afford to wait no longer. Beyond the clearing where the second man should have appeared by this time in plain sight, there was nothing moving.

'Drop the carbine,' he called.

There was a slow stiffening of the man's body from knees to shoulders. He did not obey the order.

'You drop the gun or I drop you.'

'Who are you?' the man asked, still with his back to Wheeler and therefore unidentifiable. 'Is this a robbery?'

'You know better than that,' spoke Bob divining the other man's thoughts. 'Now drop the carbine and quit stalling.'

Still there was no move on the gunman's part to let fall the carbine. 'Listen,' he said, speaking with unnecessary loudness; speaking hurriedly so that the words ran together. 'I got some money in my pocket. I'll take it out real slow and drop it on the ground, then I'll walk out of here.'

'Mister,' said Bob, his voice going softly quiet amid the trees so that it carried no farther than the man under his gunbarrel. 'Mister; he can't hear you no matter how loudly you talk, because he didn't come along the trail. Now, for the last time; drop that gun—or use it.'

At long last the stranger let go the carbine. It fell upon spongy pine needles while its owner began slowly to reverse his stance; to face towards the locality he knew now held his enemy.

The man was not Mike Barlow; he was Eb Cartwright and simultaneously with the warning flash in his head against this deadly gunman, Cartwright went for his belt-gun.

Twin muzzle-blasts exploded together. The echoes that ran tumultuously from these inseparable eruptions might have been made by one gun. Well clear of the forest where the trail lay could now he heard the run of a horse while in among the trees and east of the dying campfire there was no sound at all for a time; not until a man's emptying tones told of someone hard hit back there.

'I didn't believe anyone could be faster...'

'Let go the pistol, Cartwright. You can't lift it anyway.'

'I got a thirst, Wheeler. I'm on fire in the soft parts.'

'Drop the pistol.'

There was the echoless rustle of a heavy object settling into pine needles, then: 'God—it burns, Wheeler.'

'I'll fetch some water. Lie still.'

But Wheeler was impatient; he stood for a time near his saddle listening to the fading hoof-falls of Mike Barlow's racing mount pushing steadily southward and beyond his immediate reach. It crossed his mind to leave the dying Cartwright and go at once to conclude the business which had brought him this far from his homeland. In the end though he took up his canteen and returned to where Cartwright was leaning, propped up with no look of great suffering to him, but with the indelible shadow of death clear to see in his expression; in his dark-circled and unnaturally motionless eyes.

'It's gone now,' the dying man said, drinking a little then turning his face away from the canteen. 'The burning's gone.' He swung his head to face Bob. 'My legs are numb; they feel cold.' He took a gulp of air. 'Wheeler? It's the big one, isn't it?'

'Yes.'

'Where?'

'From front to back below the breastbone, Cartwright.'

'Well...' Cartwright broke off and started

over. 'You made good time. Mike said you'd try it; 'said you had a reputation down on the plains for never givin' up. He was scairt to death o' you, Wheeler.'

'He has a right to be.'

'Yeh. 'Killed your brother; isn't that it?'

'That's the big end of it, yes. But he killed him when my brother was unarmed. He was only a kid, Cartwright.'

' 'Never had a brother, Wheeler. It's—hard to grow up though. Hard—to do some of the things you got to do in life.'

Eb Cartwright's fading gaze fixed itself upon Bob. He sighed, the breath rattling out of him audibly.

'You know why I came out to Nevada, Wheeler? I'll tell you. Because it made me—sick—having to back up my reputation to every green kid with a gun.'

'You came out here to the same kind of thing, I'm told, Cartwright.'

'Yeah. That proves something, Wheeler. It proves what they told us as kids: leopards can't change their spots.'

'Maybe leopards don't try. 'You like another drink?'

'Whisky; if you got it. No more water.'

'I have no whisky; just this water. Want me to make you a smoke?'

'Don't smoke, Wheeler.' Cartwright brushed his fingers over the gun lying near. 'Feller once told me—Wheeler—your last little while— you think of something you'd like to have done before you cashed out.'

Bob looked briefly at the widening dark stain then dropped his head to make a cigarette.

'Wheeler? Something I'd like—take my gun. Keep it. The next time you got to kill a man take it out and look at it. Will you—do that?'

'I'll do it, Cartwright.'

'You promise?'

'I promise.'

'Good. That's what I always wanted to do; always wanted to quit—to get away—to stop; because—hell—I knew someday this'd happen.'

'Cartwright? You got folks back east or somewhere?'

'Just that louse Hal Cullen—my cousin.'

'Well...'

Cartwright understood, but his voice was blurring now, thickening as his throat and tongue failed to respond. 'Anywhere's all right with me. Just put up—plenty rocks—keep the coyotes—and wolves out.'

'I'll do that.'

Somewhere in the overhead pine limbs a bluejay screamed and scolded. Through this raucousness, closer and therefore audible, came a sighing-soft rattle; a softening of Eb Cartwright's frame, a loosening of his muscles. It could have been that he dozed in the pleasant and warm fragrance.

'Cartwright?'

Again came that scolding rasp from the bluejay far above.

'Cartwright...?' Quieter this time, gentler, along with a probing hand which felt the cooling-out of a dead man's flesh.

Bob stood up. 'Then I guess,' he told the corpse, 'it'll be right here. At least there'll be no souvenir hunters to dig you up for a coatbutton or a finger-ring or a spur strap.'

He twisted once to look out over the dwindling far grade of the *arriero* trail, then fell to work scooping out a grave, and afterwards he did as Cartwright had wished; he hauled stones to make a pile of them so that scavenging beasts would not dig up the dead man. It was by then late afternoon with a reddening sun dropping away towards a misty horizon. Somewhere ahead Mike Barlow might be waiting hopefully for Cartwright. More than likely, Bob thought as he struck camp after freeing Cartwright's horse and dropping Cartwright's gun into his saddle-pocket, Barlow was plunging headlong ahead towards the softly distant hog-back of the rising, cresting Sierras.

He rode loosely now, without spirit. There had been, earlier in the morning, a little pang of hunger in his belly. Now there was nothing in him at all; no feeling one way or another. It was enough to simply rock along with his rested mount; to become a part of this dying day. Not to have to direct the animal or consider the lead Barlow now had upon him, nor even to think—to remember.

There were, however, the unvarnished, frank and simple words of a dying man to hear faintly echoed until long after the sun settled enormously red and egg-like, upon a distant pinnacle before it burst into a thousand shattered filaments spreading its red torrent outward over a day which was also dying. He kept steadily onward projecting no defences against those words; convinced in his innermost heart of their truthfulness.

'...Hell—I knew someday this'd happen.'

CHAPTER TWELVE

Every gunman knew that some time, somewhere, he would face if not necessarily a faster
gun, then at least a truer one. The unchanging first law of survival ensured this; for when
a man reached the point where he could down
so renowned a gunman as Eb Cartwright had
been, he had arrived at that phase of his time
when the only route left for him to travel was
downward. Downward into the same kind of
a grave which Cartwright now occupied.

But this was no new consideration for Bob
Wheeler. Nor had he ever been the same kind
of a fast-gun that Cartwright had been. He had
never sold bullets nor killed without what, in
the eyes of the frontiersmen, was just and am-
ple cause. But he was, regardless, a famous
fastgun and the day after downing Cartwright—
more than ever that day—as he continued on
his private vengeance trail he knew without a
solitary doubt that soon now some other gunman, coming into his own time of brief glory,
would call him out for no better reason than
to prove himself faster, truer, or braver.

Long before he rode a tilting saddle down from the heights towards a hidden emerald valley of inviting size and beauty where a near-river freshet ran from overhead snow-caps, he had held his life to this moment at arm's length and viewed it without dishonesty, and had come to a conclusion that, while it actually did him no dishonour, neither did it do him honour.

When he came along the freshet's scored banks and paused seeking a fording place, his thoughts had turned away from a past which he had now resolved not to pursue to its obvious ending. He did not immediately find the ford but he got down to stand cleanly in dazzling sunlight and face a future which promised much labour, perhaps no great or early rewards, but which offered the quiet solitude a man needed in his life; the kind of quietude which went with a blameless conscience.

He led his horse into a thicket, made him fast there, then went belly-down to drink at the creek, wash his face and freshen the water in his canteen. It was while he was occupied with the canteen, holding it firmly in both hands, that the voice came to strike him hard in the back.

'Easy, stranger. Just sit easy there, now.'

He froze wondering at the strangeness of this

voice. It had the timbre of too many ac-
cumulated years to belong to a man as young
as Mike Barlow.

'All right,' he responded. 'I'm sitting easy.'

'So y'are, boy; so y'are. Now keep tight hold
o' that canteen with both hands an' don't make
no sudden moves.'

A hulking gaunt shadow fell across Bob
where he hunkered in the grass. When he gazed
upwards his eyes crossed the gaze of as brittle
and keen a stare as he had ever before encountered. The tall old man was dressed Indian-like,
in smoke-tanned hides and moccasins. He was
holding forth an immensely long-barrelled sixgun. He also had a rifle and a sheath-knife. At
his belt hung a greasy parfleche bag.

'I know what ye're doing here, boy, and I
don't figure it's good for a man to burn hisself
out with hate'n all. So I figure we'll just sit here
'til after dark—then I'll leave'n you can do what
you like.'

Bob watched the old man squat cross-legged.
'Mind if I put this canteen down now?' he
quietly asked.

'No; I don't mind. Just keep both hands in
front of ye, is all.'

Bob's gaze turned ironic. 'What kind of a
yarn did he tell you, mister?'

'That ye're after him to kill him.'

'Anything else?'

'That you're fixin' t'do this 'cause he bested your brother in a fair fight.'

'How much did he pay you—twenty dollars?'

The ancient trapper bobbed his head. 'Twenty dollars is right,' he said forthrightly. 'But I'd likely have done it 'thout pay. I don't hold with that kind of killing, mister.'

'Do you hold with murder?'

'None at all.'

'That brother of mine he killed, mister, was eighteen years old. He was not armed when Barlow killed him. He never in his life wore a gun.'

Silence settled. The trapper shifted where he sat; he considered Bob thoughtfully then he scowled. 'A man can get fooled,' he said finally. 'You speak out like a man tellin' the truth.'

'Then do you mind if I head out? There are still some daylight hours left.'

'I mind, boy. Like I told you—I don't hold with the kind of killin' you got in mind.'

'Do you hold with letting murderers run loose to murder again—and again?'

'Well; no; can't say as I rightly do.'

'I don't have any money,' Bob said, eyeing the trapper's threadbare appearance. 'But back a few miles there's a clearing beside the trail.

149

I left a good saddle horse, saddle and bridle there.'

'Anything else, boy?'

'Yes. A grave.'

'I see. He told me you might've downed his pardner. A good horse, mister? A good saddle and bridle?'

'Better'n I'm riding by a long shot.'

'Wish I could take you up on this, boy, but like I said, I don't hold with grudge-killings.'

Bob gazed a long silent moment at the canteen in his lap. 'Suppose,' he eventually said, speaking slowly because he was simultaneously forming an idea and a sentence. 'Suppose I gave you my word I won't shoot him on sight. Suppose I can take him alive, then return him for the law to try for murder.'

'You'll give ye're word on that boy?'

'On my word, oldtimer.'

The trapper's long stare ended abruptly as he arose, uncoiling up off the ground with the gracefulness of a man who seldom sat any other way than cross-legged. 'I'd say,' the trapper exclaimed, rummaging in his parfleche bag, bringing forth a crumpled twenty-dollar bill. 'I'd say give him this money, son. A man can't rightly take pay for something he don't do.' He hefted his rifle, staring back up the far side of the mountain. 'How far back'd ye say

150

that critter an' outfit was?'

'Eight or ten miles back. In a clearing beside the road where there's a dead campfire and a grave.' Bob eyed the other man's parfleche bag. 'You got some jerky you can spare, mister?'

With a nod the mountain man removed his bag and tossed it down. 'Smoke cured,' he said, then departed, striding strongly towards the drop-off over which Bob had recently descended into the mountain valley.

Bob carefully folded the twenty-dollar bill, pocketed it and chewed a stringy piece of jerky. He eventually returned to his horse, settled across the saddle and rode down into the freshet, across its brawling width and out upon the far side where a brief but minute examination of Mike Barlow's fresh tracks showed by their crumbling edges that they had been made less than an hour earlier.

He pushed on until shadows came, stealthily long and thin at first, then wider, deeper and bolder, to nibble away at the cooling last light of evening. He considered keeping to the trail as he had thus far done out-riding his prey by endurance alone. But in the end he did not, for the elemental reason that, knowing Barlow was very close by in the thickening gloom, he did not wish to pass him in the night. The night before, it had been different; neither Cartwright nor Barlow considered it possible for pursuit to be ahead of them. They had not watched the trail ahead for tracks. This was no longer the case; from now on Mike Barlow would keep a sharp watch earthward. He was running scairt, and a frightened man had very sharp eyes.

But the fates which had helped, then hindered, Bob's hard ride, now wearied of this sport and gave him aid. Less than six miles beyond the mountain meadow and with dusk settling fully over the peaks and forest, he scented a fresh cooking fire. The aroma of boiling coffee equally with the knowledge of who probably sat by that fire, gave his wearying spirit new life. He left his horse off the trail hobbled in a tiny clearing where bunch grass grew thickly tufted, and went softly forward on foot stopping at intervals to quarter the night for coffee-fragrance.

In an hour he saw reflected, dancing firelight where it showed above tree tops. By that time the smell was strongly borne by night air.

He came down from behind the camp site and for a time stood rock-like watching the huddled figure whose back was to him. It was not necessary to see Barlow's face; he had met the man only once on the Blockton Plains, but in a hundred visions since that time months earlier, he had seen this man's tallish frame, his narrow-featured face and his gold-flecked rebellious stare.

Barlow was eating. Across his lap lay a carbine. At his hip was a black-stocked sixgun, the little leather thong which range men kept tied over the naked bulge of their hand-guns when riding, so the guns would not be jarred from the holster, was pulled loose so the gun could be instantly drawn. Mike Barlow was, as Cartwright had intimated, apprehensively shaken.

Bob remained a long time watching his enemy. In his mind was a natural although subdued sense of triumph. It had taken a long time for him to arrive at this point, and yet as much as he wished to destroy this murderer, he found satisfaction in the thought that he would not do it as he had originally planned. Not simply because he had given his word to the old trapper, but also because he knew that a swift killing would leave him dissatisfied. Mike Barlow had to suffer and sweat and cry before he died. He had to know hope, and suffer the gradual diminishing of that hope. He must feel futility and remorse. There were crimes for which frontiersmen offered understanding, even compassion, and there were crimes for which they felt no earthly retribution was adequate punishment. Murder was such a crime, and in Nebraska—Bob Wheeler's mind, the murder of his only living relative, an eighteen-year-old unarmed boy, was just such a crime.

His thinking, while standing fifty feet behind Mike Barlow, took a cruel shape on his mouth; it burned with unrelenting ferocity in his stare. And when at last he spoke, his voice was thickly menacing; the words fell like iron balls striking glass, turning Mike Barlow to stone with their deadly promise.

'Barlow; don't move!'

There came to Barlow's narrow shoulders a gradual stiffening; a twitching. He expected fully to feel the crash of a bullet into his spine. Where firelight flickered over his face reddening it, there was the faintest narrowing of nostrils; the slow-widening of eyes that mirrored complete desperation; near-panic. Barlow scarcely drew in any breath at all.

'Take up that carbine left-handed and put it out on the grass away from you.'

Barlow obeyed like a man in a trance.

'Now the sixgun—left handed, Barlow, and real slow.'

Unlike Eb Cartwright who, being a gunfighter, thought in terms of resistance, Mike Barlow, basically a coward and a craven, gave up his sidearm with emerging hope; he knew,

154

no matter how much a man wished to kill another man, he would not do it if the other man was unarmed. With elaborate slowness he obeyed Bob, placing the pistol at the farthest distance of his outstretched arm. Then he folded his hands in his lap, waiting; breathing better now, his colour slightly returning, beginning to hope, beginning to craftily speculate on Wheeler's intentions.

'You got a boot-knife, Barlow, or a derringer?'

'No. Just the carbine and hand-gun, Wheeler.'

Bob went silently forward, around the squatting man.

'You wouldn't know me by my voice,' he said, easing down beyond the fire, catching Barlow's gaze and holding it. 'So it must be your conscience that told you who was behind you.'

'I knew, Wheeler. I knew last night when Eb didn't return. There was only one man in the Kearney country who might've bested Eb Cartwright.'

Bob reached into a shirt pocket, drew forth a smooth and sweat-darkened wallet and tossed it across the fire. It fell within inches of Barlow's folded legs. He gazed at it blankly.

'Pick it up,' ordered Wheeler. 'Look inside it.'

'Why? It's some kind of a trick.'

'It's your brother's wallet, Barlow. I figured you'd guess what happened if you saw his wallet. A man doesn't give up his wallet unless he can't help himself.'

Mike Barlow made a slow examination of the wallet. He fingered its contents and put it gently back upon the ground.

'Did you kill him, Wheeler?'

'I killed him.'

'And Cartwright?'

'You've guessed about that. I buried him, too.'

'And—me?'

Before replying Bob let his hand-gun off cock and holstered it. 'That'll be up to you,' he said. 'You can take up your pistol if you want to. I'll even let you try for it where it's lying— without holstering it.'

But Mike Barlow shook his head; he was not afraid, he was simply unshakeably convinced of the foolishness of such a move on his part. 'No,' he told Wheeler. 'There'd be no point in me trying that against a man like you. If you figure to kill me you'll have to do it like I'm sittin' here right now. I'm not going to make a play against you, and that's my final word on the matter, too. You can't force me to draw and you can't bait me into it.' Barlow's voice gathered strength. 'I'd ride all the way back to Kearney with that gun loaded an' in my holster—and you couldn't taunt me or feint me into drawing it against you, Wheeler.'

Bob did not speak again. Instead he bent from the middle, took Barlow's cup of hot coffee, sipped it, and while new life was warming his body and invigorating it, he also ate Barlow's prepared supper of fried beef and Indian cabbage. Afterwards he made a cigarette and gazed upon his prisoner.

'It's a long way back' he said, and noticed the instantaneous loosening of Barlow's body at his words; the brightening of sly hope in Barlow's gaze. 'You lie back if you're a mind to, and get some sleep.'

'You're not going to tie me?'

Bob arose, went around the fire and picked up Barlow's weapons. 'You might want to make a run for it in the night,' he said, smiling steadily down at his prisoner.

The murderer's perplexity gradually turned sardonic. He lifted an ironic gaze to the man standing over him. 'Oh no,' he said. 'You are not going to get a chance to shoot me, Wheeler. You can't make me draw against you, and you can't tempt me to make a run for it.' Barlow settled upon the ground with his face towards the diminishing fire, a very faint, bitter small

157

smile around his lips.

'You can go back in the trees and watch me all night, Wheeler, but I won't give you the excuse you want. Not by a damned sight.'

Bob also made a mirthless faint grin. Then he went back, took Barlow's horse through the forest where his own animal patiently waited, hobbled both horses and returned. He emptied his guns as well as the guns of Mike Barlow, cached the slugs and made a pine-needle bed. He lay down and instantly slept.

CHAPTER THIRTEEN

Before first light Bob was poking up the fire, stirring coals and bringing them to new life with more faggots. Then Barlow sat up, made a face and spat aside, Bob held forth his hand.

'This is your twenty-dollar bill,' he said. 'I've got a feeling it'll be the last bill this size you'll ever own.'

Barlow took the money and examined it. Then he stuffed it carelessly into a pocket. ' 'From the old trapper?' he asked.

Bob nodded. When the frying meat and coffee were ready he said, 'Have a good sleep, Barlow?'

'Yes, I had a good sleep.' Barlow's whiskery face split into a taunting smile. 'You didn't get your chance, did you, Wheeler?'

Bob shrugged, pushed a tin plate and cup across the fire and said, 'I don't know whether I had a chance or not. I slept like a baby.' He lifted a slow long glance and lay it upon Barlow. 'You could've run, I wouldn't have known it. You could've brained me with a rock, too, for that matter.'

159

Barlow's stare held steadily to his captor's face; he read the truth there and his cheeks filled with angry dark blood. He ate without speaking and afterwards made a cigarette. He finally said sullenly and without conviction: 'I still wouldn't have tried it.'

Bob ignored Barlow and re-loaded his pistol. This, more than his words, seemed to convince Barlow that Bob had indeed slept instead of standing guard over him through the dark hours. He said two savagely profane words and lapsed into a stony, bleak and furious sulk which was not broken for hours after they were on the trail; was not broken in fact until, half a day later, Bob reined up beside the clearing where Cartwright's stony cairn lay in full sunlighted view of the route they were traversing.

Cartwright's saddle was not where Bob had left it. He leaned down from the saddle to make out moccasin-sign. It was there. He looked at Barlow, whose fascinated gaze clung to the grave.

'The old boy in the antelope-skin britches was here. I gave him Cartwright's horse and outfit.'

Barlow looked away from the grave. He had heard but did not heed his captor's words. 'He caused all this,' he exclaimed, speaking of dead

Eb Cartwright. 'He did Cullen's thinking and planning. Except for him I wouldn't be in this fix now.'

'Did he make you go to the Blockton Plains, Barlow? No; he had no hand in that, and that's what I wanted you for. Not for the rustling or even for the burning of New Hope. Those things weren't my fight—until Keystone made it that way. Then I had to beat Keystone to get at you.' Bob nudged out his horse. 'Move on,' he said, 'and quit feeling sorry for yourself. A man's responsible for his own failings after he commences shaving, Barlow. You've been nothing but a tinhorn since you were old enough to strike out on your own.'

Barlow rode ahead, slump-shouldered, silent and trail-grimed. His mind refused to project itself ahead; there was no hope in that direction; it continued to dwell upon the past; upon the things which, had they happened differently, might have permitted him to escape the situation he was now in. Before evening he said to Bob: 'The kid made me do it. I'd had a few drinks. He made fun of me 'cause I lost the card game.'

Bob's shifting gaze fell upon Barlow's back and did not move away. He said nothing, just let the contempt, the scorn and relentless hatred burn there.

161

'Wheeler?'

'What?'

'Is there anything I can say; anything I can do?'

'No; there is nothing. A few months ago there might've been, but now there is nothing.'

'Money, Wheeler...?'

'No.'

'I deserve a chance, Wheeler.'

'So did the kid. So did the squatters. I imagine, in your lifetime, Barlow, there've been lots of folks who also deserved a chance. They didn't get anything from you so what makes you think you've got anything coming?'

'You're condemning me. You know that, don't you?'

'Barlow,' said Bob wearily, with settling night closing down. 'Why don't you shut up? I gave you a chance last night. You were too yellow to take it; you wouldn't even raise up and look around. If you want, I'll give you back your hand-gun...'

'No. I told you I wouldn't draw against you.'

'Then quit whining about me not giving you a chance; I've offered you one.'

'That's no chance. That'd be murder, Wheeler.'

'It would be a better chance than you gave my brother. Now shut up, Barlow. I'm sick to my stomach of you.'

Nothing more was said between them until midnight, then Barlow wanted to know when they were going to stop.

'We aren't,' Bob told him. 'You stood the gaff on the way out—you can stand it on the way in. If you get sleepy, get your rest in the saddle. I did that tracking you; it's not hard to do.'

They bored steadily onward through screening darkness. Bob chewed smoke-cured jerky and smoked the last of his tobacco. He had no great difficulty in keeping awake; he was, like most range men, a person who could get by upon a minimum of rest; the sleep of the night before had been adequate. Barlow, too, despite what he said, was not a man who required much sleep; he rode along now drowsing in the saddle.

When the brightening new warmth of a fresh dawn rolled downward from the heights filling their silent world, Barlow called back: 'You're going to kill these horses, Wheeler.'

'We're going to stop directly,' said Bob, his mind previously made up concerning this. 'You want some jerky?'

Barlow slowed his mount and held forth his hand. When he had the parfleche bag he studied it, then looked swiftly up into his captor's face. 'The old trapper, too?' he asked breathlessly. 'Did you kill him too?'

'Don't be silly. He gave me that bag. I told you yesterday I let him have Cartwright's outfit.'

Barlow took some jerky and handed back the bag. 'I guess I didn't hear you,' he said. He swore at the memory of the mountain man, then.

'Dirty old traitor. I should've shot him.'

Wheeler's hard glance fell upon Barlow. 'In the back,' he said. 'You'd have to have done it that way, Barlow, because he was armed.'

Barlow fell into another dark sulk and for once Bob wished this was not so because the burning sun was upon them with its full blasting heat and it was harder now to remain awake than it had been in the coolness of full dark.

He sought for something to close his thoughts around; something that would vitally hold his interest. Instantly the vision of Aimee McDonald came to him. The drowsiness fell away then.

He recalled without difficulty her steady gaze; the way her expression had faintly changed, on the steps of the church; the fullness of her lips and their yielding heaviness under his own mouth.

He was so absorbed that he did not at once place the voice that came to intrude upon his reverie; not until Mike Barlow's rising words struck against him with their triumphant ring and surging hatred.

'Draw up, boys.'

He looked around and down with a physical effort, pulling his thoughts back to the present with an effort.

'I said draw up there.'

It was Barlow's identifying cry that brought his attention fully to the afoot figure in the shade at the side of the trail, with its cocked pistol and its waning grin.

'Jeb! Damn it all Jeb I was never so proud to see a friend in all my life. Shoot him, Jeb. Shoot the murdering skunk out'n his saddle.'

Jeb was watching Bob with sun-squinted eyes. He flagged at him with the pistol, ignoring Barlow's cries.

'Get down, boy,' he ordered Bob. Then, with Barlow piling off too, his face flushed with a vast relief, the old rider backed off and swung his sixgun. 'Quiet down,' he told Barlow. 'Just stand back there with Wheeler and quiet down.'

Perplexity settled down over Barlow's face. His mouth hung open. 'What the hell,' he murmured, gazing upon old Jeb Arbuckle with increasing puzzlement. 'What's got into you, Jeb?'

'Lead them horses in here off the trail,' ordered Arbuckle, and moved aside as his captives obeyed. 'Now Wheeler—shed that pistol.' When this too had been done, old Jeb sank down in the shade, motioning for Barlow and Wheeler to do likewise. He mopped sweat off his face with a grimy sleeve and lowered his gun.

'You got *him*,' he said to Wheeler, eyeing Bob carefully. 'What about Butch and Eb?'

'He killed 'em,' shrilled Mike Barlow. 'Killed 'em from ambush, Jeb. In cold blood.'

Bob ignored Barlow and kept his eyes fully on the old man's face. When Barlow finally subsided he said, 'What's on your mind, Jeb? I reckon you know there'll be a posse behind you somewhere?'

Jeb grinned at that, his face splitting up into dozens of tiny hair-lines. 'Assumin' I did like you asked me to,' he replied. 'Told them lawmen what you asked me to tell 'em.'

'Didn't you?' asked Bob, with a sinking heart.

Old Jeb merely shrugged his shoulders and continued to study his prisoners. After a time he said to Bob: 'How'd you best Cartwright? I know how you downed Butch. I know 'cause

I rode through that old ghost town yesterday an' the fellers there was havin' the time o' their lives. Seems like nothing as interestin' as a gen-u-wine gunfight has happened there in thirty years. Now then—what about Cartwright?'

'It was a fair fight, Jeb,' answered Bob. 'I was standing half behind a big fir tree. Otherwise there'd likely have been two dead men back in those mountains instead of one.'

'Jeb,' burst out Mike Barlow, his voice made sharp by impatience and desperation. 'What's the matter with you? I used to be a Keystoner—remember? You're a Keystoner too. Shoot this damned Nebraskan and let's get out of here.'

' 'Tain't gentlemanly,' the old cowboy told Barlow, broadening his enigmatic smile, 'to shoot an unarmed man, Mike. Even you know better'n that.'

Bob, watching Arbuckle closely, got the idea old Jeb was deliberately prolonging this meeting. But he could not, for the life of him, imagine what was behind Arbuckle's grinning countenance. He thoughtfully plucked a blade of grass and began chewing it. The longer Arbuckle held them there the greater was the possibility that riders would come up and find them. This of course brought him face to face with the old cowboy's remark about the Kearney posse; if Jeb had not passed the word as

Bob had asked him to do, then their wait might indeed be a long one.

He finally cut across Mike Barlow's continuing and indignant pleadings for Jeb to shoot him, saying, 'Out with it, Jeb. What's on your mind?'

Arbuckle's fading smile instantly firmed up; a craftiness appeared in his eyes. 'Now you're talkin' sense,' he exclaimed. 'Boy; I once done you a favour, didn't I?'

'You did.'

'An' being a fair-minded man—as well as sudden death with a hand-gun—you'd be willin' for an old man you owe a favour to, to cash in just a mite if he got the chance, wouldn't you? I mean, boy, I'm an old man. I'm not here for long. You can see that an'—'

'You're going to make me weep,' interrupted Bob. 'Get to the point, Jeb. I'm dog-tired and I want to make Kearney before nightfall.'

'If there was a reward on Mike here, and also on Butch and Eb—would you be willin' for an old man to have it?'

With the coming of understanding Bob put a long, sardonic gaze upon the old cowboy. Instead of answering the question he said dryly: 'Mind if I pick up my gun now?'

At this Barlow made a final impassioned outburst. Jeb and Bob ignored him and Arbuckle

168

self-consciously holstered his own weapon. He said, 'I had to try it, boy. I had to because this'll be the last chance I get to pocket a sizeable wad of money.' Jeb seemed thoroughly subdued.

Bob took up his gun, blew dust off it and holstered it. 'Jeb,' he said, 'who put up this reward and when did they do it?'

'Two counties: Kearney and New Hope. They went together on it three days ago. That's when I started after you.'

'You didn't tell Jack Martin or Charley Crowninshield where I went, when I asked you to?'

Old Jeb squirmed. 'Well; it wasn't exactly like that, boy. You see; when they got their posse together I seen they had four old Keystone riders among 'em. I was scairt to step out into the roadway, like, and tell 'em in front of them men. Anyway; before I could make up my mind they lit out like a herd of fresh-cut calves.'

'So they don't know I'm up here.'

'They know now, boy. I run across Aimee McDonald whilst I was ponderin' over what to do, an' told her. She said she'd go after the posse and tell Charley and Jack.'

'Then you rode hell-for-leather up here to get here first?'

'After I learnt the re-wards was gen-u-wine.'

Bob held forth his hand. 'Tobacco, Jeb,' he growled, and when the old cowboy handed over his sack with alacrity Bob went to work. Without looking up he said, 'You doggoned old fool.' He lit up, exhaled and tossed back the sack. 'Jeb; before I'd have let you free Barlow I'd have made a jump for my gun. I guess you never in your lifetime came closer to dying than you have today.'

'You wouldn't have,' said old Jeb. 'Not with my gun on you, boy. You're too smart for that—even if I wouldn't have fired on you.'

'You wouldn't have fired on me, Jeb.'

'No; but you didn't know that.'

'Yes I did.'

'How,' challenged Arbuckle.

'Jeb; look behind you. No; the other direction. See that long-barrelled rifle on your shoulders?'

Arbuckle saw the mottled, shadowed musket. Barlow saw it too. Until that moment neither of them had any idea the three of them were not alone in among the trees. Jeb's breath whooshed out in a pinched-down loud sigh.

Bob called out: 'Come on out, oldtimer. I owe you something for that.'

The mountain trapper appeared, his gun held across his body in both hands. He looked with glowering disapproval at the blanched and perspiring countenance of old Jeb Arbuckle. 'A man your age,' he intoned dourly, 'ought to have more decency in him, stranger. If you'd just looked like you was fixin' to pull that trigger I'd have blown your skull apart like bustin' an over-ripe melon.'

CHAPTER FOURTEEN

Bob was dehydrated and tired. Beyond that lay some kind of unpleasant feeling. He said nothing until the mountain man had dropped down cross-legged amongst them, holding his long-barrelled old musket so that its over-size opening was less than a yard from Jeb Arbuckle's middle.

'I'll he'p you take them in,' the trapper said, ignoring Barlow in favour of Jeb. 'I'm disappointed in a man like this older one,' he intoned. 'A feller grows older, he's supposed to get wiser. This one's nothing but an old fool. A silly, sly old fool.'

Jeb's colour left. He avoided that fierce and towering contempt which was being bluntly turned upon him. Bob, watching, felt a little saddened; a little compassionate. It must, he thought, be the worst kind of gall to grow old; to be treated as something no longer useful, no longer worthwhile, in a land where once a man had ridden proud in his saddle.

'No,' he told the mountain man. 'I thank you, but I won't need help taking Barlow in.

As for Jeb—hell—he can have the rewards.'

The trapper accepted this magnanimity with a wag of his head and a scowl of solemn approval. 'But he should be taught a lesson, too,' he mumbled, bending his bleak stare upon Jeb again.

For answer Bob got up, went to his drowsing horse, brought something forth from his saddle-bag and returned to them with it. He tossed it lightly upon the ground. It was Eb Cartwright's empty sixgun. Barlow's eyes recognised it instantly and remained upon it in a spellbound way.

'The man that gave me this gun,' Bob said, 'was not a good man, I reckon, but when he was dying he was at least for that little time a wise man.' He touched the gun with his fingers. 'He didn't tell me how a gunman must end up; he didn't even say gunfighting was wrong. All he said was for me to keep his pistol and if I was ever again called upon to kill another man, to take out his pistol and look at it.' He caught the trapper's knowing gaze and nodded into it. 'I see you understand. Well; that reward money's going to work on Jeb the same way. Every time he takes up a dollar of it, he's going to remember something that'll make him think a little less of himself. What more punishment can one man give another man?'

The trapper lifted his gaze from Cartwright's pistol and lay it forthrightly upon Bob Wheeler. 'I got to tell you something, too,' he said. 'I didn't just happen to be back in them trees, mister.' He cleared his throat taking his time with the words he needed to continue speaking with.

'I figured yesterday you were a truthful man. But I'd been wrong with the other young feller, so I concluded to find out who was a liar and who wasn't.'

'You waited along the trail to see if I'd keep my word to you,' Bob stated. 'To make sure I'd bring Barlow back alive as I said I would.'

'Yes.'

Bob's lips curled a little at their outer edges. In a quiet way he said, 'Mister; I'm right glad you did. I'm sure Jeb wouldn't have shot me, but I'm not so sure Barlow here might not have tricked him and got his gun, in which case I would have been shot.'

The old trapper came up off the ground. He leaned upon his musket gazing at the three of them. 'Sometimes folks wonder why a few of us still live out in the mountains,' he exclaimed, speaking quietly. 'All they got to do is be around *people* long enough and they can figure it out for themselves.' He drew up, threw Bob

174

a curt nod, and faded out among the trees.

For a while longer Jeb and Mike Barlow sat stone-like. Then Bob said, 'Get your horse, Jeb. I'm tired enough to fall asleep in the saddle. You can spell me off keeping an eye on Barlow.'

They rode out upon the trail in deep silence as far as the ghost town. There, Bob led them circuitously around through the moutains so that they avoided that place, and afterwards, with afternoon light steadily failing, he kept on without a pause in spite of Mike Barlow's frequent sullen glares, until, after midnight some time, they left behind those secretive mountains and came down upon the powdery land running dead-flat as far as Kearney and much farther.

Jeb was in galled torment by sunrise, his meatless shanks unaccustomed to this killing pace. But he held his tongue, until, with the others ready to fall from their saddles and the hoof-falls of their mounts dragging, scuffing up floury dust, Kearney was in sight, and this side of it several miles, the kicked-up dust-banner of many oncoming riders. Then the old cowboy drew upright with an effort and reached over to shake Bob awake in his saddle.

'Posse's on ahead,' he croaked. 'Seems to me they might've made better time'n they did.'

Bob rubbed his face with fisted hands. 'They had Cullen and the cutting crew to round up first.'

But Jeb was not placated by this and snorted, 'Eb an' Butch was the important ones. And Mike here, too, I reckon,' he added; then doubtfully, 'although I'm not so sure about Mike.'

The possemen swirled up and for a space said nothing; Bob and his prisoner were fiercely unclean, gaunt and half-dead looking. It was Charley Crowninshield who recovered first from his shock and spoke.

'He'd have been better off if you'd killed him,' he said to Bob. 'Here; I got a bottle of whisky.'

Bob refused the drink. 'Give it to Jeb,' he said, 'he's older and probably needs it more.'

Crowninshield obeyed and Jeb drank.

Jack Martin looked with puzzlement upon the old Keystoner. 'How come you to be with Wheeler?' he asked. 'I figured that you'd left the country, Jeb.'

'He helped me bring Barlow in,' Bob cut in to say.

At this Mike Barlow turned a dull eye upon Wheeler. But he said nothing.

They reached Kearney with the moon's later rising just beginning to throw out soft light.

Barlow was taken to the jailhouse and Jeb Arbuckle disappeared into the night.

Bob told Kearney's lawman, Jack Martin, everything that had transpired since last they had been together, and Charley Crowninshield, when Martin protested about giving Jeb the reward money, sided with Bob.

'Like he says,' the New Hope lawman stoutly said, 'even if old Jeb didn't have any part in the trailin' or gunnin', Wheeler wouldn't have been able to fetch Barlow back because he was out on his feet for loss of sleep. So—'

'All right,' Martin agreed, but without very good grace. 'It's Wheeler's word, an' that's good enough. Old Jeb get's the money.'

As though from a distance Bob heard himself asking: 'What of the others; Cullen, Turk, Dusty...?'

'All accounted for,' said Charley Crowninshield, gazing long upon Bob's face. 'That's what delayed us comin' up into the mountains after Aimee told us. Got every last one of 'em. Cullen's in Jack's jail. Would you like to see him? I imagine he'd be interested. You're the man who shot it out with his famous cousin and walked away alive. Cullen'd like to see the man who did that.'

'I don't want to see him.' Bob sucked back a big breath and faced Jack Martin. 'Something you could do while I'm catching up on my sleep,' he said.

'Sure; just name it.'

'Wire the sheriff of Blockton, Nebraska. His name's Tim Beasley. Tell him I got Barlow. Ask him to wire extradition papers.'

Martin and Crowninshield exchanged a look. Martin said, 'I did that. Not about the extradition papers. About you. Why didn't you just come right out an' tell us you were a deputy sheriff under Beasley?'

'Didn't he tell you why I couldn't do that?'

'No.'

'Because I couldn't call Barlow out and kill him with a badge on my shirt. That's why. I took a leave of absence.'

'But you didn't call Barlow out.'

'I meant to, sheriff. I never meant to do anything so much in my life.'

Crowninshield stirred; he shifted his feet and he stood with an unasked question poised upon his lips. Bob understood Crowninshield's expression. He deliberated long over his answer, then he said, 'A man can't ever go over the same piece of trail again. But before it's too late he can turn onto the trail he ought to ride. I didn't kill him because that's up to the law, not me.' He fixed them both with his tired eyes. 'Eb Cartwright before he died, had a part in making me see that.'

He left them standing upon the dark plank-walk looking after him, entered the Palace of Pleasure and went steadily to the bar. The barkeep, a paunchy man with a soft round face in which lay no great show of character, wrinkled his nose. Bob saw this and considered it. He afterwards said, 'Mister; a cool glass of beer. No; make it two. And mister—' as the barman moved to comply, 'if you wrinkle up your nose again I'm going to put two bullets in you. One between your eyes and one where the third button down is, on your shirt.'

Around him men drew away, some looking back with hard interest, others startled and wishing only to get clear. One of the latter, a merchant with sky-blue sleeve-garters stopped Jack Martin who was just entering, and said swiftly, 'You got a bad one there at the bar, Jack. A real bad one. There's something in him that's about to make him do a killing.'

'Naw,' contradicted Martin, seeing who the merchant was looking back at. 'He's just worn down to nothing but nerves and guts. That's the man who outfought Eb Cartwright and buried him.'

The merchant disappeared into the night with a choked-off gasp. Other men, hearing Martin's casual words in the sudden silence, left the Palace of Pleasure without a second glance backwards. Sheriff Martin smiled; he chuckled and stopped to lean upon the bar next to Bob. To the barman, whose face was suddenly terribly white and loose-hanging, Martin said: 'Get the boy something to eat, Earl. Don't just stand there shakin' in your boots. This man needs food and lots of it.'

When Sheriff Martin emphasised his point with a struck-down fist upon the bartop, the fat man jumped, then moved swiftly towards the far end of the counter.

Bob ate and drank until even Martin was astonished at his capacity. Then he called for a cigar, lit it, savoured the sharp bite of good tobacco, and leaned there looking vacantly at nothing.

After a time he said, 'I got to have a bath, a shave, and some fresh clothes.'

'Sure,' agreed Sheriff Martin.

'What time is it?'

'Gettin' on towards ten o'clock.'

Bob rummaged for some coins, put them upon the bar and left the saloon. He went to the hotel and ordered a bath. It was half after ten o'clock when he reappeared upon the plank-walk cleansed, freshly attired, full of food and now only a little less dead-tired than he had earlier been. He could not have explained what it was that drove him to this thing he was now embarked upon; he could just as well have done it the next day or the next evening.

He strode westerly down the star-hung night and paused within sight of the McDonald house. It glowed soft-silver in the lighted night and he stood there, more at a loss than he had ever before been in his lifetime. A wraith of paleness came down from the porch of that white house and came steadily onward to him. He had his eyes full upon it and heard as though from a goodly distance the words that reached ahead to him.

'I heard you were back,' Aimee said, coming to a gradual halt yards away; watching his night-shadowed lean strong features. 'I'm glad it ended for you this way.'

He felt around for his new tobacco sack and looked away from her, bringing up his hands automatically to fashion the cigarette. 'What way?' he asked her.

'Without killing him.'

He lit up, inhaled deeply and exhaled, still looking beyond her to the high yeasty starshine where it merged with earth at the horizon's far curving.

'Why should that matter to you, Aimee?'

'You could have killed him easily enough. I know about you now, Bob.' She took one of

181

his hands and led him unresistingly to the porch steps and there she put him gently down with her hands and sank down beside him.

'It mattered to me because...'

'Yes,' he urged her, leaning back, looking out upon the night.

'If you had killed him it would have simply meant that you had learned nothing in those mountains. That you were the same man you've always been.'

'How do you know what kind of man I've always been?'

'When a man never changes, Bob, it means he's always been as he is. That he won't change.'

'And that is bad, Aimee?'

'It can be. Eb Cartwright couldn't change. A man with a gun for his only friend...'

'Goes from bad to worse?' he finished for her, making a question of it. 'Can't change?'

'Yes.'

He turned towards her and solemnly put out the cigarette. He could feel more than simply her nearness; he also felt the wave of warmth coming from her and going into him, drenching him with its sweetness and its discontent.

'You could be right,' he said to her, and for a full minute afterwards added nothing to it. Then he said. 'Cartwright knew, though. He knew before he died.'

She murmured up to him: 'Did he have to die to find it out, Bob?'

'I think he did, Aimee. Maybe men learn things like that pretty slow.'

'Is it like that with you, Bob?'

'No.'

'And now; now that you've learned—what next?'

'I don't know.' He looked down into her face. 'Right now I'm too tired to think about it, Aimee.'

'You didn't think about it on the trail back?'

He said to her again: 'I don't know. Maybe I did. Maybe even before that—after I'd buried Cartwright. I was restless and dissatisfied.'

She put forth a hand to let it lie gently upon him. 'I had my thoughts too,' she murmured. 'While I waited for you to come back. I had them while I rode after the posse-men and sent them to you.'

He squared towards her recalling their kiss. Her face tilted a little but she made no first move towards him. He reached out and touched her; felt the solidness of her flesh beneath his hands and drew her to him. She came without resistance but also without eagerness. His head went low and for a moment he saw her full mouth below him where it trembled, waiting, the lips minutely parted. He kissed her and in that interlude there came from her a rush of strong passion; enough to tell him that here was no girl, here was a full woman.

They parted.

She smiled into his eyes. 'I think if you had not come back to me tonight, Bob, I would have died.'

'We've only been together once before, Aimee.'

'You're tired,' she told his lips, her eyes upon them. 'You're tired or you wouldn't confuse time with something that has nothing to do with time.'

'But I'm a stranger here too.'

'What's that got to do with us, Bob?'

'This is your town—your country, Aimee.'

'It's all the same country, Bob. If you want to take a fresh trail I'll follow you.'

He brushed her mouth with his lips then drew fully away. 'The restlessness is gone, Aimee. It's completely gone.'

She said nothing, only watching him in the soft-pale night.

'I guess maybe it wasn't Barlow or Cartwright or anything else that troubled me. It was you.'

'Then you have no longer any troubles,' she said, continuing her study of his strong face.

'Put your head back, Bob.'

He obeyed her, thrusting his legs out to their full length and letting his body run loose upon the porch steps. She cradled his head and when she spoke a while later, he made no response. He was deeply and exhaustedly asleep.